PROTECTED BY HER BODYGUARD

EMILY HAYES

Emerald Crowle opened the door to the backseat of a shiny, black Bentley. Before extending a long, lean leg out of the car, she turned to her driver, Jesse. "Thanks so much. I'll see you at 5:00 am tomorrow."

The driver kept his eyes on the front window, replying obediently, "Yes, of course, Ms. Crowle. I hope you have a lovely evening. I'll be waiting at the gate by 4:45 am."

"Perfect; I love your punctuality. Goodnight, Jesse." Emerald slid out of the luxury vehicle, moving directly to the entrance of her Beverly Hills mansion. The sun had just begun to set, casting a warm glow upon the property of the grand estate. She was glad to be returning home before nightfall; luckily, her scenes in the upcoming movie had been scheduled in the early morning. But considering the stature of this world-famous actress, Emerald wouldn't have had it any other way.

At this point in her career, Emerald Crowle called the shots. It was well-known that any director who wanted to work with her needed to concede to her schedule and preferences. But that was hardly an issue for anyone working in the Hollywood film industry; the 58-year-old actress controlled the box office, and if she starred in the leading role, the money would roll in. Her stunning beauty was the main attraction in any movie, and her longevity within the industry had cemented her as an icon.

Her patent-leather Louboutins click-clacked against the cobblestone pavement leading up to the front door. Before Emerald could reach for the doorknob, her housekeeper, Marilyn, greeted the actress. "Good evening, Ms. Crowle. How was your day? I've prepared your evening tonic; it's waiting for you in the parlor."

Every evening, Emerald enjoyed a cup of Jasmine Silver Needle tea, an expensive and rare blend containing anti-aging properties. She believed this ritual helped to maintain her glowing skin and youthful appearance. Based on the reviews of the thousands of adoring fans, the tea was working in her favor.

Marilyn Jefferies had worked for Emerald Crowle for over twenty-five years; she had been hired once Emerald first achieved success and fame as a Hollywood star. Marilyn had seen Emerald throughout all of the drama of her career, including her multiple marriages. She was a staple at the estate, and of all of the people who worked for Emerald, Marilyn was a grounding force who was considered family. No one was closer to the actress, not even her third husband, whom she was currently divorcing.

"Oh, that's wonderful. Thanks, Marilyn. Did Rudy call?" Emerald was referring to her lawyer, Rudy Cohen. Mr. Cohen was the most high-profile lawyer in California, and his legal prowess was considered a threat within the courtroom. Rudy had represented Ms. Crowle in her previous divorces, so naturally, he was her only choice regarding her current split.

"Yes, Ms. Crowle, he did. I left the message on a notepad beside your drink. He knew you would be tired after being on set all day, so he asked if you could call him in the morning." Marilyn helped Emerald out of her Mulberry silk coat as the actress set down her mandarin-colored Birkin purse.

She strolled down the hall, entering the parlor; this was her private sitting room for when Emerald sought solitude. Occasionally, Marilyn would host a formal afternoon tea for Emerald's close friends, but generally, this was the place where Emerald could be alone with her thoughts. She sat in her favorite embroidered antique chair, illuminated by an overhead Tiffany lamp. Her tea was set off to the side on a marble table, and a notepad beside it.

Emerald looked at the scrawled notes Marilyn had transcribed from Mr. Cohen and smiled. It was just as she suspected; her prenuptial agreement was solid, and whatever claims her soon-to-be ex-husband made would never hold up in court. Breathing a sigh of relief, Emerald sank deeper into her seat, feeling satisfied and triumphant.

Ah, yes. Time to decompress, Emerald thought to herself. *I suppose I should call Marty about changing the lines in my script. He knows I would never agree to such language.*

The actress had struggled through the

dialogue in her newest film, mainly because the text didn't resonate with her. But Emerald knew she was no longer in a place where she needed to settle. She had paid her dues within the industry and could now be more selective. Moreover, given the respect that she has earned over the past thirty years, she was well within her right to request changes from her director.

She took a few delicate sips of her tea before turning on her private Smartphone to message the director the required edits. But as soon as the device powered up, Emerald noticed a string of new text messages, appearing one after another. *Ding! Ding! Ding!*

Emerald's stomach sank. *Fuck! It's Thomas. Rudy must have contacted Thomas's lawyer to tell him about the prenup. Oh no, this is bad.* The actress took a deep breath, preparing herself for the tsunami of anger that her former husband had been known to unleash. While she didn't want to read his texts, Emerald knew that the messages could serve as evidence in case she needed to take legal action. Her stomach lurched as she thought back to the past clues that hinted at Thomas's temper, and Emerald chastised herself for not taking his erratic emotions seriously.

Emerald Crowle had met her third husband, Thomas Black, while preparing for a movie called *Fire in Heaven*. Emerald played an assassin, Angela, who was seeking revenge on the mobsters who murdered her father. The role was physically demanding, and her agent had introduced Emerald to an up-and-coming personal trainer in Hollywood.

Even though he was new to the industry, Thomas had already built a reputation as a tough, no-nonsense coach who had previously been in the Marines. While his client roster was small, demand for his classes quickly increased among actors who needed to get into serious shape. Emerald required top-tier contacts known for their excellence, so naturally, Emerald chose Thomas Black as her personal trainer.

Their fitness sessions were intense, and Thomas was both extreme in his methods and emotions. But Emerald failed to see the warning signs because she was focused on achieving physical superiority. But there was another aspect to Thomas that drew Emerald in, and that was his growing popularity as the new "golden boy" in Hollywood. The athletic trainer was very handsome, catching the eye of every female A-list celebrity. Thomas Black was a hot commodity at the time, making him a must-have for Emerald even though she was a lot older than he was.

Emerald knew exactly who to surround herself with to deflect any attention from her deepest secret; Emerald Crowle was a lesbian. She had spent many years expertly hiding this fact. It had been made clear to her in the early days of acting that coming out as gay would have killed her career. So, instead, Emerald surrounded herself with very attractive men, and as her success and fame grew, it was very easy for Emerald to snag a pretend husband. In fact, she was so good at it that she married twice before meeting Thomas Black.

Secretly, Emerald had taken many female lovers over the years. She only chose to sleep with women who weren't public about their sexual orientation throughout her 30 years in the film industry. This way, she trusted, they also had reasons to keep her secrets. Whenever she was done with her current husband, Emerald filed for divorce, knowing that her air-tight prenup would keep her safe from gold diggers. Split marriages were so common in her industry that it almost became a trend. And she was also aware that any man who was associated with her would receive instant fame himself. So Emerald justified her behavior because the arrangement was transactional for all involved.

However, unlike the more passive men that Emerald positioned herself with, Thomas Black was an incredible force. At his best, he was passionate and engaged, but his dark side was aggressive, unpredictable, and sometimes terrifying. At first, Emerald tried to ignore his growing agitation and emotional instability because, from the start, she was never emotionally involved.

But one evening, after Emerald had returned late from being onset, she came home to find the foyer of her mansion trashed with broken artifacts and clothing strewn about. Thomas was furious that Emerald wanted to break up with him. She would never forget the moment Thomas lurched towards her, punching a hole in a wall inches from her face. Emerald immediately called private security and filed for divorce the next day.

The months that followed had broken Emerald's spirit. She was constantly inundated with threats, with Thomas showing up unexpectedly on set. Finally, Emerald threatened to file a restraining order against Thomas, which seemed to calm the situation. It had been at least a month since she heard anything from him. But upon receiving his texts, Emerald knew that she was in trouble, especially because he was not legally entitled to any of her assets or wealth.

Swallowing hard, Emerald clicked on the first message.

You fucking bitch! You're going to pay for this! You haven't heard the last of my lawyer...or me!

With a trembling hand, Emerald tucked a piece of golden-blond hair over her ears and bit her lip. She took another deep inhale before opening the second message.

I hope you sleep well tonight, bitch. It would be a shame if someone was to sneak into your window and put a pillow over your face while you're sleeping. I'm sure you have nothing to worry about, though, right?!

"Jesus Christ, he has gone off the deep end," she whispered to herself. Emerald was a strong and confident woman who was not easily intimidated. But Thomas was going too far.

I've been tracking your whereabouts. How's the new movie going? Do you like shooting at the Hillside Studios? I know you thought I wouldn't find out the location but guess what, bitch?! I'm fucking smarter than you. Maybe I'll make a surprise visit and blow the whole place up. How would you like that?

Emerald closed her eyes, feeling nauseous. The movie set was supposed to be top secret; only the crew involved in the film knew where Emerald was shooting. It made her sick with worry that Thomas found out about the Hillside Studio location.

At this point, Emerald couldn't read any more messages. She sat frozen in the parlor for what seemed like an eternity, feeling her world crash around her. She tried regulating her breath to calm her thoughts as she formulated a solution.

"That's it; I'm done with being harassed. If this fucker wants a fight, he will meet his match," she tersely wished out loud.

Upon making her decision, Emerald immediately called her agent, Chet Walker.

"Chet. I'm still getting threats from Thomas. I need you to get me a bodyguard. Female. Capable. The best there is."

Emerald would not waste one more moment, especially with these threats. An empowering force rose within her; *no one messes with me, especially an overgrown child like Thomas Black. This is war.*

_____

2

Sweat collected around Romy Russell's hairline as she flung herself up to the steel bar, kissing it with her chin. *Argh, 42 reps... must get to 50...* Her biceps contracted as she slowly lowered herself, feeling her legs dangle near the ground. Romy could feel teardrop-shaped beads begin to fall in her eyes, but she was undaunted. A fire grew within her trapezius muscles as she blinked; her body raged with an insurmountable force.

Romy loved to start her morning with an intense workout; the physical burn and tenacity required fueled her mental clarity, leaving her focused for the day ahead. Grunting, she rose up once again for another pull-up. With every pull-up, she was driven to do more, almost as though she was obsessed. Given that it was only 5:00 am, the 24-hour, private gym was completely empty, but that was precisely how Romy preferred it. She revelled in solitude, with the sharp sounds of her breath being the only sounds.

Most members of Thor Fitness, located in the posh neighborhood of Beverly Hills, didn't arrive until 6:30 am, but most guests did not lead the life of Romy Russell. Typically, the fitness center was populated with famous models and working actors led by their private trainers. But the 38-year-old bodyguard was in a league of her own. Considering that her work hours were long and unpredictable, Romy dedicated the wee hours of the morning to her physical training so she could enjoy the solitude before the space filled with others.

"Come on; you can do this!" Romy spoke aloud to herself, pushing through to meet her max capacity. "Ahhhh, yes!" Her bony chin hit the steel bar for the last count of 50 as Romy dropped to the ground, her feet firmly planted on the mat. Keeled over, Romy took a few breaths, wiping the sweat off her face and running her hands through her short, dark-brown hair. "Oh my god, fuck, that was intense!"

Unwrapping the gauze from her hands, Romy sat down on a bench to drink, sipping cold water from her thermos. Her head tingled with endorphins, and her heart rate slowly returned to normal. Blinking, she looked around the expansive weight room, catching her reflection in the mirror.

In general, Romy wasn't overly concerned with her appearance, but she did notice that her hair needed a trim. *Jesus, I need to get this mop fixed up.* She rubbed the back of her neck, feeling the stubble from her undercut. Romy loved the new razored cut, which perfectly suited her soft butch style. But as a famous bodyguard to A-list celebrities, Romy always needed to appear tidy and polished. Like her clothes, Romy's hair had to be serious and conservative, but that suited her fine; it was an aesthetic that had always resonated with her.

Given that Romy Russell had trained at a police academy in Houston, Texas, before becoming an officer for five years, she was accustomed to discipline and structure. Romy was also a fierce competitor and overachiever. At 22 years old, she received a degree in Law Enforcement, with a follow-up degree in Criminal Justice two years afterward. Romy was the youngest person in her program to complete all of the required qualifications to enter the police force. And for a few years, she enjoyed her work.

But Romy was an ambitious woman, and soon, she became bored with the daily routine of her duties. Nevertheless, Romy craved excitement and a challenge, and after taking a year off to weigh her options, she decided to move to California and explore a career as a bodyguard. Her fierce commitment to physical superiority and her natural ability to problem-solve under pressure made her an excellent candidate. Soon, Romy rose within the ranks of the premier company Panther Security International.

At this point in her profession, Romy was well sought-after with a solid reputation for being one of the best bodyguards within protective services. Considering the hectic—sometimes chaotic—lives of many of her clients, Romy had seen her fair share of conflict. However, she was an excellent mediator, confidant, and assertive with a weapon when a situation turned grave. But unfortunately, Romy's personal life was not as prolific.

Whenever Romy was assigned a client, her

entire attention was focused on their protection; this meant that personal relationships needed to take a backseat. Romy was also required to travel constantly, accompanying her high-profile customers wherever they needed to go.

Romy was a handsome woman; extremely fit, standing tall at six foot one, and her ice-blue eyes were nothing short of mesmerizing. At first, the women who came into Romy's life were impressed, even attracted to her career. But typically, after a few months of dating or communicating long-distance, her girlfriends would become frustrated with Romy's frenzied schedule and lack of romantic attention. Romy desired love and companionship, but she knew it could never come between the life and well-being of a paying client. At this point, she was resolute on remaining single, at least until she was done with her career.

Moving through her high-intensity interval training, Romy crouched down to grab a set of coarse, thick ropes. Taking a few deep breaths, she faced herself in the mirror and honed her focus like a tiger. This was an exercise that Romy enjoyed timing, challenging her momentum to beat the time from before. *1, 2, 3, go!*

With aggression, Romy began to shake the

ropes, whipping them hard against the matted floor. Her muscles burned with a glorious ache that fired her competitive spirit. Within a minute, her reflection served a glistening body, highlighted by sweaty shoulders and pulsating forearms. Adrenaline fueled Romy through her workouts, losing herself to the moment. Considering the bodyguard needed to be alert at all times while on assignment, Romy relished the times when she could let go of her mind and let her body take over.

This morning had been like so many recent mornings. Finally, Romy found herself with more time to spend at the gym and also to enjoy the fruits of her labor. But she never wanted to remain idle for long. It had been almost three weeks since she had been assigned a new client from Panther Security International. As much as she appreciated the rest, she was eager to return to the field and excel at what she did best.

The *ding* of her phone signaled that Romy had reached her time on the ropes. Wiping her brow with a towel, she sauntered over to her device. A text appeared with the contact noting the security agency. Romy whispered joyfully to herself, "Yes,

I've been waiting for this!" She opened the message and read its contents.

As her eyes traveled over the words, Romy felt slightly deflated. *Hmmm, okay. Emerald Crowle the movie star, huh? Getting threats from her ex husband? hmmm.*

Celebrities were never the favored clients for most bodyguards. Too much drama, attention seeking and diva behaviour made a bodyguard's life difficult.

Like the rest of the world, Romy Russell was well-versed in the public life of Emerald Crowle. And while she had never worked with the iconic actress, she had many past clients who knew her. From what Romy observed, Ms. Crowle brought out intense emotions in people. Depending on who it was, she either instilled complete adoration or menacing hatred, the latter being her ex-husbands. While Romy never wanted to judge her clients, she couldn't help categorizing Emerald Crowle as a diva.

Still, I want the work. Hmmm, alright. Yeah, I'm going to take this assignment. I mean, how hard can it be? I've taken on more than just squabbling ex-lovers. I think the only challenge is enduring entitled, prima-donna behavior. Romy called Panther Security to

3

"Marilyn!" Emerald called out in a forced, singsong voice. Now that Emerald found herself alone, once again, at her private estate, she yearned for attention. Unfortunately, the way that Emerald expressed her need for closeness was through giving orders to her help. Because Emerald had spent her entire adult life in the spotlight, surrounded by an entourage of assistants, many of her interactions involved giving or taking direction.

But Emerald had much love for Marilyn, and throughout her years of fame, she considered the housekeeper as the only family she truly had.

Emerald was aware that her diva behavior could push others away. Lately, she had become more mindful of her tone and attitude, although at 58 years old, changing old habits wasn't always fruitful.

She could hear her housekeeper rummaging through some boxes in the next room, but Emerald was currently putting on her makeup, choosing to summon the help into her bedroom. "Marilyn? Hello? Could you come here, please? I need you!"

Within seconds, the housekeeper appeared, looking flushed. Apologetically, Marilyn replied, "Yes, ma'am. I'm sorry, I didn't hear you. I was just clearing the boxes out of the spare room." The elderly, ruddy-faced woman wiped her hands on her denim jeans and beamed at her employer. "What do you need, my dear?"

Keeping her eyes glued to her reflection, Emerald ran a fluffy makeup brush across her high cheekbones. Then, smiling at Marilyn through the mirror, Emerald answered, "Is the guest room prepared adequately? Romy Russell, the new bodyguard, should be arriving soon. I want to make sure she has everything she needs."

"Yes, ma'am. Her bedroom has been prepared.

I just need to throw out the debris. Then, I will prepare a light lunch in the formal dining hall."

Marilyn stood obediently, her hands folded in front of her plump tummy. "Do you have any meal requests?"

Emerald brought a single, manicured finger to her lips in thought. "Hmmm, good question. Let's do a lobster ceviche. Oh, and please chill a bottle of champagne." Satisfied with her decision, Emerald continued to focus on preparing her face.

The housekeeper was never one to question her boss, but Marilyn's brown furrowed slightly. Then, timidly, she asked, "For the bodyguard, ma'am?"

Emerald froze, biting her lip with a frown. But after a few seconds, she burst into laughter. "Oh, goodness! I suppose you are right—how silly of me." Then, meeting Marilyn's reflection, Emerald reconsidered, "Please offer Ms. Russell some sparkling water with lunch. But *I* will have a glass of champagne. That will be all." Emerald winked at the housekeeper, dismissing her from the bedroom.

Emerald knew that she shouldn't be drinking during the day, but given the continuing threats from Thomas, Emerald had been on edge. At this point, she was becoming fearful of leaving the house, which was an issue given that Emerald was in the middle of shooting a film. But she had every reason to be afraid.

Even thinking back to the other day, Emerald remembered receiving a bundle of packaged flowers while on set. The gift was addressed to her, so there was no reason for the crew to open the wrapping. At first, Emerald was delighted, as she assumed the flowers were from an adoring fan.

But upon opening the wrapped package in her trailer, Emerald discovered that the bouquet was actually a bunch of dead flowers. She gasped aloud and dropped the roses as her heart pounded in her chest. *Oh my god! He wasn't kidding when he said that he knew the shoot location. Thomas Black could find me anywhere.*

Being a consummate professional, Emerald was able to continue filming with the crew that afternoon. Still, as soon as the day was complete, she wanted to hide alone in her mansion. Some of the other castmates had invited Emerald to join them for cocktails, but she politely refused. The only place she felt safe these days was at home with her loyal Marilyn.

Studying herself in the mirror, Emerald

noticed the signs of worry and aging on her porcelain skin. Then, sighing out loud, she spoke quietly to herself, "Gosh, this bodyguard can't come soon enough!"

Emerald heard the doorbell within seconds of summoning her desires to the Universe. Leaving Marilyn to welcome the bodyguard, she took a few more minutes on her appearance. Emerald wanted to appear composed, calm, and beautiful as the superstar that people expected her to be. But on the inside, Emerald was shaking.

Slowly, Emerald made her way down the grand staircase. She noticed Marilyn facing a woman with dark hair in a ponytail and broad shoulders, although Emerald couldn't make out her features.

Emerald cascaded down the stairs. "Hello! Sorry, I was just upstairs, getting ready to greet everyone." As the statuesque brunette turned to face Emerald, she felt her eyebrows raise and a flush run over her cheeks. *Are you kidding me? Holy shit, this bodyguard is hot!* Emerald was never at a loss for words, but the sight of this athletic and handsome woman caused her to freeze momentarily.

As she reached the ground floor, the bodyguard approached Emerald. "Hello, Ms. Crowle.

My name is Romy Russell, and I've been assigned to your case." Romy stuck out her hand, gripping Emerald's in a strong and confident hold.

Emerald felt herself blushing. "It's a pleasure to meet you, Ms. Russell. My, that is quite the handshake you have!" Emerald was immediately in awe of her. Romy reminded Emerald of Demi Moore facially, but with a more muscular and towering build. Her blue eyes were piercing and her gaze confident as Emerald released her hand.

Emerald immediately felt giddy, recognizing her nervousness as an attraction. It had been a long time since a woman made her feel so demure. Typically, Emerald was the one in control, using her charm to seduce a lover that was starstruck by her status. And usually, any woman she had been intimate with was more feminine. Emerald concluded that because women in Hollywood needed to assume a distinct look to be hired, most of her lovers had a similar appearance; augmented breasts, Botox, and hair extensions were common. But Emerald definitely had a *thing* for more masculine women, and her first impression of Romy threw Emerald off guard.

"Thank you, ma'am. I hope I didn't hurt you. Sometimes, I don't know my own strength."

Romy's eyes twinkled warmly, but her expression remained serious. "Although, in my line of work, it's important to keep fit and strong."

"Oh, I'm sure it is. You look like you are in excellent shape, so I'm sure I'll be in good hands." Emerald grinned suggestively, well aware that she was flirting. Within the many years of her career, Emerald had never required such a level of protection. Of course, she wasn't sure of the correct protocol when dealing with a bodyguard, but Emerald didn't see the harm in enchanting her guest.

But Romy was nonplussed, maintaining a solemn expression. "Yes, ma'am. I also come with years of experience. Your agent, Chet Walker, explained your situation. I also received details from the private security company. I'm hoping that my services will help keep you at ease."

To Emerald, Romy seemed impossible to read, and she wasn't used to having her flirtations dismissed. Unsure what to do next, Emerald looked helplessly at Marilyn for direction. Picking up the cue from her employer, Marilyn beamed, "Ms. Russell, I'd love to show you to your room. After you are settled, we'll enjoy a light lunch. I've prepared something special for you to welcome you to Ms. Crowle's estate."

"Thank you, that sounds good. I will need to check in with the company to inform them that I am now on location," Romy replied. Marilyn smiled. "Of course, dear. I'll grab your belongings while we travel to the second floor."

Romy paused briefly before adding, "I appreciate that, but I'll need to take one of the bags myself." Romy pointed to a lengthy, black oversized duffle. "This bag is specifically for my guns, so I should handle this myself."

Emerald's eyes widened while Marilyn assumed a stoic yet warm expression. "Of course, my dear. Whatever you prefer, I am just here to help. Please, follow me." As Romy and Marilyn traveled up the stairs, Emerald began to feel overwhelmed. Her mind was spinning over how attractive her bodyguard was but also because of Romy's weapons. Having armed security in her home now made the stalking issue much more real, and Emerald now understood how dangerous her situation had become. Feeling restless, she padded into the formal dining room, waiting for Romy to join her. Emerald was pleased to see the elegant settings around the large oak table. She wanted to make an impression on her new guard, especially after noticing her physique and exquisite features.

Emerald felt herself oscillating between stress and excitement. *Well, at least I have a sexy body-guard in this large, empty mansion to keep me company. Who knows? Maybe we will become friends. Or maybe friends with benefits...*

Emerald was lost in her thoughts when she noticed Romy leaning in the dining hall doorway. "Hi, ma'am, um, or Ms.Crowle. Is this where you'd like to discuss the case?"

As Marilyn followed quickly behind, scurrying into the adjacent kitchen to prepare lunch, Emerald smiled coyly, summoning Romy into the room. "Yes, please sit." She pointed to an empty chair directly across from her. "Marilyn is making us something special to welcome you to my estate. I thought we could enjoy a meal, and I could learn more about you." Emerald bit her lip, grinning suggestively. "Do you like ceviche?"

Romy sauntered over and sat, facing Emerald. Her expression was cool and detached, although Romy's ice-blue eyes possessed an astute and clever awareness. Emerald hoped to charm the bodyguard with her signature grace and elegance, but Romy appeared untouchable. *Hmmm, I do enjoy a challenge! I wonder what she would be like in bed. Intense, vivacious, maybe even passionate? Butches always seem so cold until you warm them between the sheets!*

"Sorry, ma'am, what's that?" Romy asked, furrowing her brow. "I mean, I like everything. I don't have any allergies if that's what you're wondering?"

Emerald laughed gently. "Oh, it's a cold seafood dish. This one is made from fresh lobster hand-picked from the ocean today. Oh, and please, call me Emerald," The actress licked her lips, maintaining her gaze on Romy. "I'd love us to be friends if we can."

To Emerald's delight, Romy gave a slight smile, displaying a dimple on her left cheek. Then, while she avoided Emerald's intense stare, Romy chuckled. "Alright, I'm cool with Emerald. And I guess you can call me Romy, so we're even. We will be working closely together."

"Good, good, that's what I like to hear." Emerald cooed as Marilyn placed a glass of champagne in front of her. She looked up to nod at her housekeeper while Marilyn provided Romy with sparkling water.

"Thank you, ma'am, that's perfect. I don't drink

alcohol, but I am parched." Romy raised the glass to her lips before Emerald stopped her. "Oh, I was sure that you *didn't,* so I instructed Marilyn to bring you some Acqua di Cristallo; it's the Rolls Royce of seltzers.

Raising her champagne, Emerald announced, "Let's have a toast! To my new friend Romy; may she keep me safe from my terrible ex husband." Winking, she clinked Romy's glass as her eyes traveled from her face to her biceps, which seemed to burst through her black, tight-fitting T-shirt. "You *definitely* seem up for the role."

Clearing her throat, Romy replied, emphasizing her professionalism, "Yes, to keep you safe, which is *my job.* But Ms.—oops, I mean, *Emerald,* I would like to give you some guidance and recommendations in your situation. Okay? I'm as serious as a heart attack regarding your protection, so you must heed my words."

Emerald felt a thrill as Romy finally looked her in the eyes. Nodding eagerly, she leaned in closer. "Oh yes, of course. Please, I'm all ears."

Straightening her posture, Romy began, placing her hands on the table. "First, I will need to accompany you everywhere, regardless of whether it's a social visit, a party, or a gala. I want to be no further than fifteen feet away from you, although in some cases, I will be right beside you." Romy stared at Emerald to ensure that she understood. "I will also be joining you while you are filming on set. Obviously, I won't interrupt any scenes or be in the way but my presence will be known."

Emerald bobbed her head, drawn to every word. While she listened, Emerald kept her eyes on Romy's full lips, imagining what they would feel like on her own. "No problem, I understand. And yes, I would love that." As soon as her words escaped her mouth, Emerald realized that she sounded a little too excited to be followed by a bodyguard, but her lack of shame allowed Emerald to brush off any self-consciousness.

Romy continued. "Second, I will need to have access to all of your husband's personal and professional information, including any special contacts, messages, threats, anything and everything. Part of my process is to do a thorough investigation. I need to see *everything.*" Emerald nodded, averting her eyes as she remembered Thomas' sinister texts. A slight fear entered her heart, making her feel vulnerable.

"And third, I'd like to sleep in the bedroom

next to yours. It's essential that I am close in prox-
imity. Will that be an issue?

Emerald shook her head. "No, not at all! In fact,
the bedroom Marilyn assigned you is directly
beside mine. So don't worry; we'll be close."

Very close, I hope.

4

Romy pulled her black SUV into the long, winding driveway of Emerald's estate, pausing to announce her return through the gate's intercom. Static, followed by a fuzzy robotic voice, came through the speaker.

"Hello. Please state your name and purpose for visiting Ms. Crowle." To Romy, the announcement sounded automatic, as though the gate was operated by a comprehensive security system.

Rolling down the window, she replied, "Yes, hello? This is Romy Russell. I'm Ms. Crowle's bodyguard." Romy waited a few seconds before the arm on the gate turned green, raising itself so that Romy could drive through the gate. But then, she thought, *Hmmm, that thing is not safe. I'll talk to her about a more advanced security system. I mean, I could've been anyone; it just let me in.*

The sun was rising in the sky, lifting the darkness of night, announcing that morning had arrived. Romy had awoken to her alarm that was set for 5:00 am. At first, she was disorientated but then remembered her assignment. It wasn't unusual for Romy to wake up so early, especially when she was working with a client. The early dawn was usually the safest time for Romy to work out at the gym because, in her experience, most criminals were not active during those hours and most clients weren't up then either. Usually the client's bed was the safest place for them.

Grounding herself in a new working environment was essential for Romy's focus. But this morning, instead of Thor's Gym, she decided to visit the QuickSilver Shooting Range to practice a few rounds. While most gun ranges were closed at this hour, Romy had gotten special access due to her status. (and Emerald's money.) She wanted to prepare herself for trouble, but Romy still wasn't convinced that Emerald was in grave danger. To Romy, the actress seemed like a superficial and slightly lonely woman who tried her best to draw attention with her looks and artificial charm. Romy had met many A-list actors within her career that reminded her exactly of Emerald. Still, she seemed pleasant enough, and the housekeeper was a real gem. Romy figured that this was going to be an easy enough assignment, and she was content with her conclusion.

Romy entered through the side door of the mansion as instructed; the property was ominously quiet. *It's only 7:10 am; Emerald must still be sleeping.* This morning, she wanted to start the investigation process into Emerald's ex-husband, Thomas Black. In addition to physically protecting her clients, Romy also conducted a thorough inquest into known adversaries. Romy knew that having a better understanding of the threat meant that she could better track his moves.

Procuring a laptop from her room, Romy moved downstairs to the dining room to begin her morning work. As she settled into a cushioned seat, she couldn't help but chuckle under her breath, remembering Emerald's flirtatious behavior. There was no doubt that Emerald was extremely attractive; Romy's preference had always been toward older women. And like most beautiful celebrities, Emerald led with her sex appeal, which was initially entrancing. But soon, the act would wear thin, exposing a deeply insecure person who desired attention. Given Romy's past experiences, she was no stranger to female clients coming on to her, but Romy never became intimately involved; it was terrible for business and bad for her concentration.

Just as Romy was plugging in her devices, she heard rustling from around the corner. "Hello and good morning, dear! Did you sleep well?" Romy immediately grinned at the sound of Marilyn's voice. Then, standing from her seat, Romy went to greet the elderly housekeeper.

"Good morning, Marilyn. I did, thank you. The room is beautiful and comfortable. I was just out at the range to practice with my gear." Romy was always careful not to go into too much detail about her weapons, which intimidated most people. Besides, Marilyn was such a kind woman that Romy felt just as protective of her as she did Emerald Crowle.

"That's nice, dear. Would you like some coffee? Can I make you any breakfast?" Marilyn asked. "Emerald is typically awake by 8:00 am on the days she is not on set. I'm about to make eggs benedict if you would like that. But let me know; I could make anything you want really." Marilyn beamed, proud of her skills.

"I'd love some coffee, but I'm alright for breakfast; thanks for offering," Romy replied politely. Inside, she was surprised to hear that Emerald woke as early as she did. Given her flighty behavior, Romy assumed that Emerald slept until noon and enjoyed breakfast in bed.

Suddenly, Romy heard a voice from upstairs. "Marilyn? Marilyn, could you come upstairs, please?" Romy turned to see the housekeeper rush up the winding staircase to attend to the actress, and Romy rolled her eyes. *Yup, just as I suspected, a diva.*

Romy shifted her attention to the brief she had obtained from Panther Security, in addition to notes provided by Emerald's agent, Chet Walker. Soon, she became so engrossed in the details that she didn't see Emerald approaching her from behind.

"Boo! Ha ha! I hope I didn't startle you. But you looked so serious that I couldn't resist." Romy felt immediately overwhelmed by the seductive scent of Emerald's perfume. She jumped in her seat and quickly turned around to see Emerald standing behind her chair in a red silk teddy with a matching robe. She looked strikingly beautiful. Her golden blonde hair was loose and slightly tousled around her shoulders. She wore no makeup. She was every inch the movie star. Romy didn't like being snuck up on, although the sight of Emerald's beauty made her feel less pissed off.

Wryly, Romy addressed Emerald. "Actually, you did startle me. Which might not be a good idea for your safety! Please don't creep up on me like that again. Given that I'm an armed and athletic woman, it's best not to give a sneak attack." She added, in a softer tone, "How are you feeling this morning?"

Emerald reached her arms over her head, stretching her body like a cat. Her full breasts rose with her chest. Romy entirely failed to keep her eyes off them. "Hmmm! I slept *so well*. Ever since you arrived yesterday, I've felt much calmer. I think it's the best sleep I've gotten in weeks." Emerald gave Romy a warm smile. "Did Marilyn offer you anything to eat? I thought we could have breakfast together."

Romy instantly picked up on Emerald's coquettish behavior. Romy couldn't deny that Emerald intrigued her, but she was determined to remain professional. *So naturally, I should keep my distance, although there's nothing wrong with being friendly and polite. After all, this is probably the highest-profile client I've had in my career; references from Emerald Crowle would set me up for life.* Romy looked at Emerald out of the corner of her eye, noticing her curves and lovely body that was emphasized by the silky red material. *She certainly is easy on the eyes.*

"I'm not so much a breakfast person; coffee is my first meal of the day," Romy replied, holding up her mug. "But if you have something, I'm happy to keep you company. In fact, we should continue to talk more about Thomas. I have some interesting findings that you should be aware of."

"Alright, that sounds lovely. I'll have Marilyn make me a plate, and I'll join you in *just* a few moments." Emerald winked at Romy as she glided out of the dining hall. Romy kept her eyes on her keyboard, but something stirred inside her, distracting her attention from the laptop screen.

While Romy continued to investigate Thomas Black, she heard murmurs of Emerald and Marilyn from a nearby room. Romy settled in and honed her focus. Part of her research involved inputting the details that she received from the agency into a criminal database. As she reviewed the information, Romy's eyes widened. *Oh no, this is bad. Huh, I didn't realize that Thomas Black was such a threat.* She continued to read the reports that popped up from the archives. Shaking her head, Romy finally understood why Emerald required her assistance; she was concerned for the actress's safety.

Luckily for Romy, Thomas Black was not the most threatening criminal she had encountered in her career. Instead, she was well-trained and experienced, using her intelligence, skills, and strength to protect her valued clients. But Romy needed to share this new information with Emerald immediately.

Looking around the empty dining hall, Romy decided to find Emerald. Marilyn rushed into the room to check on the guard as she stood. "Is everything alright, dear? Can I get you anything else?"

"No, thank you, Marilyn. However, I do need to speak to Emerald immediately. Do you know where she is?" Romy inquired.

Marilyn pointed towards the staircase. "She's upstairs. I was just about to prepare her breakfast. Would you like to wait for her down here?"

While she felt a sense of urgency, Romy didn't

want to impose on Emerald's morning routine. "Um, sure. Yes, I can wait. I'll be waiting—"

"Okay, I'm ready!" Both Romy and Marilyn turned to see Emerald gliding down the stairs, still wearing her red silk robe, although Romy noticed that she had fixed her hair and added light makeup to her face. "Romy, you had better stay right where you are."

As Marilyn hurried back into the kitchen, Emerald took a seat beside Romy. Romy could smell the faint scent of designer perfume. *I know that smell. It's the same perfume a woman I used to be seriously into wore. Chanel Chance, I think?*

Romy assumed a solemn expression. "Emerald, I need to share some information with you; it's about Thomas Black, and it's serious."

The actress placed a hand on Romy's forearm, squeezing it. Romy wasn't sure how to react; her clients had never touched her. But Emerald's hand felt warm, sending a wave of energy through Romy's body. If Romy was completely honest with herself, she didn't mind, although she didn't want to feed Emerald's ego with a reaction.

"Goodness, what's that? What do you mean by serious?" Her hazel eyes became fearful as

Emerald bit her lip. Again, she squeezed Romy's arm, leaving her hand on the flesh.

Clearing her throat, Romy turned to her laptop screen. "As it turns out, your ex-husband has some interesting associates. How much do you know about his past?" As Romy looked back at Emerald, she met the actress's gaze. Again, they locked eyes, and Romy was overcome with a giddy sensation. *What is wrong with me today? Romy, focus!*

Slowly, Emerald's eyes traveled toward Romy's mouth as she licked her lips. Shaking her head slowly, Emerald replied, "Um, not much, I guess. I know that he was in the Marines, and that personal training was his life, but he was also passionate about acting. He was always bitter, being seen as a low-budget star." Emerald tucked a strand of golden-blond hair behind her ear and added, "Oh yeah, he became a big drinker during our marriage, and that's when he became more aggressive." Bringing her face closer to Romy's, Emerald suggestively raised an eyebrow. "Why do you ask?"

I swear, this woman could look sexy blowing her nose. She still seems composed, even flirtatious for someone with such a dangerous ex. Who is this woman, anyway? But Romy kept her expression even. "Listen, your ex-husband has former gang ties. He is associated with one of Southern California's most vicious criminal organizations. But that's not all."

Emerald put a hand to her chest and gasped, clearly shocked. Then, as her jaw dropped, she shook her head, grabbing Romy again with both hands. By her expression, Romy believed that the actress had been none the wiser; the way Emerald grasped her seemed to suggest that Emerald wanted an embrace. But Romy wasn't here to provide comfort as much as she was here for protection.

She took Emerald's hands and slowly guided them away from her body. "It's true. But I don't want you to panic. I'm getting familiar with this organization, so that I can be prepared. But you need to understand that Thomas may not be acting alone. It's possible that he could enlist in his contacts to co-ordinate an attack on you.

Romy settled back into her seat. "This is why it's imperative that I remain by your side. Today, I will locate his vehicle and put a tracker on it so I can be aware of his whereabouts."

"Of course, yes, no problem. No, I want you here at all times." Emerald appeared distraught, and for the first time, Romy sensed a genuine vulnerability in the actress. "Are you okay?"

Emerald shook her head. "No, I'm not. This is seriously worrying."

Worry lines etched over her face and for once she looked genuinely vulnerable. Her hazel eyes looked up hopefully at Romy.

Was it real or just the gifts of a talented actress?

Romy felt overwhelmed with a desire to hold her. But she knew that that would be entirely unprofessional.

She settled for putting her hand on top of Emerald's immaculately manicured soft hand.

"I've got this, Emerald. You can trust me to keep you safe." Romy hoped sincerely that her words would prove true.

Emerald's hand was warm under her own. Emerald offered a weak smile.

"I trust you," she said.

5

"Thank you so much, Heather. That looks beautiful!" Emerald admired her stylish up-do in the mirror. This afternoon, she had an appointment at Verve Salon, a posh location reserved for celebrities and significant players within Hollywood. Tonight was a special occasion as Emerald was attending an exclusive performance at the Amelia Caruso Opera House, and she wanted to look her best.

Emerald looked at Romy, seated in a chair in the waiting area. As Emerald expected, Romy needed to accompany her to the appointment. Typically, Emerald preferred to do her personal errands in private. But considering her plight and her attraction to Romy, it was a pleasant change to have company.

Poor woman, she looks so bored! I should do something to cheer her up tonight. Romy sat patiently, her eyes glued to a random fashion magazine. But as Emerald studied her hair, turning her face to the side, she caught Romy looking at her in the mirror's reflection. They locked eyes for a split second as Emerald smiled, causing Romy to look away. *Hmmm! Well, at least I know she's paying attention to me. It will be fun to tease her a bit—I mean, what's the harm?*

Heather clapped her hands together, beaming at the actress. "You look stunning, Emerald. It's always such a pleasure to see you." As Emerald stood, the hair stylist removed her cape. "What's the occasion?"

Emerald strolled towards the front area to pay for her service, and at the same time, Romy stood to move beside her. Opening her designer wallet, Emerald replied, "Tonight, I'm—or rather, I should say *we*—are attending the Amore Faralla Opera. The tenor, Maria Bartolli, personally invited me. We've known each other for *ages*," Emerald purred as she pointed to Romy. "My goodness! Where are my manners? I forgot to introduce you; this is my associate and new friend, Romy Russell."

Emerald was not yet at the point where she wanted to reveal that she had a bodyguard. Luckily, most people in Hollywood were shallow enough not to ask questions. Emerald was also known to be seen with different people, depending on the occasion, so the fact that she had brought a new face to the salon was nothing new.

Romy politely extended her hand. "Nice to meet you."

Heather replied, "Hi, Romy. Emerald has been coming to my salon for *years*. I hope you enjoy the show." Then, turning to Emerald, Heather added, sounding sympathetic, "Listen, I'm so sorry to hear about your divorce. How are you doing?"

But Emerald waved off Heather's concern. She didn't want anyone to feel sorry for her, and she certainly wasn't going to discuss the threats or imminent danger. "Oh, I'm *fine!* As the world knows, this isn't my first divorce. He was a jerk anyways." Then, dismissively, she brushed off the topic.

Heather leaned in, placing a hand on Emerald's arm. "Well, my husband Frank just hired the most handsome lawyer at his firm. So whenever you are ready to jump back in the saddle, so to speak, give me a call, and we can set you both up on a blind date." Her stylist winked, giving Emerald a nudge.

Internally, Emerald cringed. She had no interest in dating a man that served no purpose outside of appearances. If Thomas weren't so aggressive, she would have been elated about the divorce; the only thing holding back her happiness was the ongoing threats.

For now, she was happy to fly under the radar and be seen as straight. That perception was valuable to Emerald's career, and while she often entertained the thought of coming out in her later years- she knew the world was changing, she wasn't quite ready. And aside from the female, fly-by-night lovers of her past, Emerald had not yet met a woman that would have inspired her to turn her life upside down; coming out was not on Emerald Crowle's agenda.

"We'll see; I'll keep you posted," Emerald casually replied. Thanking the stylist, she and Romy left the salon to prepare themselves for the opera. As they strolled down the sidewalk, Emerald turned to Romy. "Have you ever been to an opera before?"

Romy looked at Emerald; their height was similar, allowing their eyes to meet easily. "No, I haven't. But I've been a bodyguard to a performer, and I've been backstage as security."

Emerald tittered. "Well, this won't be the same kind of experience, I can tell you that. I have my own VIP box seat and security for that section. So, you can sit back and enjoy the performance." Then, pausing for a moment, she added, "I mean, I know you are technically working, but I want you to take it in."

Romy shrugged and grinned. "Okay! Of course, my focus is on your safety, and I want you to relax. But I'm sure it will be interesting. What is the opera about?"

Emerald was pleased to see that Romy was warming up in her presence. She seemed more at ease with Emerald. It had been almost a week since Romy moved in, and the pair had developed a nice routine. However, Emerald could tell her charms were having an effect on Romy, and it tempted Emerald to test the powers of her seduction.

Placing a hand on Romy's shoulder, Emerald leaned in. "Well, it's *quite* a story! The lead character—or tenor, as she is called—Elizabeth

Carrington, is a Queen in the 18th century who falls in love with her servant Harmony. The Queen can't reveal her love because the Court would behead her. But Elizabeth and Harmony have a torrid love affair, in secret." Emerald lightly squeezed Romy, feeling the firm muscles beneath her cotton shirt.

"One day, Elizabeth and Harmony decided to travel to the countryside to enjoy a picnic by the lake. Elizabeth decides to go skinny dipping in the lake, and Harmony joins her. But a strong undercurrent sweeps up Elizabeth, and sadly, she ends up drowning." Emerald pauses and looks down at the pavement. "Sometimes, I feel like Elizabeth, actually."

The actress could feel Romy's eyes on her and sensed curiosity from her. Secretly, Emerald was hoping that Romy would question her statement. She often felt lonely in her feelings, more than anyone in her life knew.

In a way, it was safer for Emerald to confide in a stranger than her closest friends. Everyone she knew was involved in her industry and everyone wanted a piece of her fame and fortune.

But Romy replied, chuckling, "Is that the whole story? I guess I got the spoiler alert!"

Emerald couldn't help but laugh. "Well, the opera is in Italian, so you wouldn't have known what was happening anyway unless I told you. So now, you can follow along and enjoy the music and the stage." She playfully tapped Romy. "You should be thanking me!"

But Romy, who possessed a quick wit, quipped, "We'll see about that. How about this? I'll thank you for introducing me to something new, and you can thank me for protecting you. That way, we are even."

"Hmmm, I'm not so sure about that. I prefer to have the upper hand." Emerald winked again, giving Romy another light squeeze before they called the driver to take them home.

The women went to their respective rooms to prepare for the evening. As Emerald slipped her body into a long, black ball gown with a daring slit up the side, she couldn't stop thinking about Romy's strong physique and piercing blue eyes.

She imagined Romy beside her, with a firm hand resting on her knee, inside their private box seats. Emerald thought about what it would be like to feel Romy's lips on her neck as her hands slid up her dress. Her body came alive, and wetness grew between her legs. Fanning herself in the mirror,

Emerald resisted the urge to pleasure herself while getting ready. Even at 58 years old, Emerald's sex drive was still revving, and she loved to simmer in her desire.

Adding her signature cherry-red lipstick, she surveyed her appearance once more before exiting her master suite. Emerald looked down the hall, wishing she could peek inside Romy's quarters to watch her dress. But as someone who often fought for her own privacy, she decided to wait in the parlor for her bodyguard. Then, running into Marilyn, Emerald requested that the housekeeper serve her a dirty vodka martini while she waited for Romy and her driver, Jesse Stone.

"Here you go, my dear. I hope you have a lovely evening." Marilyn sat the cocktail on a table next to Emerald. "When are you leaving?"

"Jesse should be here in about fifteen minutes. Romy is going to follow behind us in the SUV." Emerald took a delicate sip of her martini just as Romy appeared in the doorway. The actress nearly choked on her drink when she saw her handsome bodyguard dressed in a tuxedo. *Holy shit! She looks incredible!*

"How's this? I figured it was best to dress formally." The suit was tailored to fit Romy's body perfectly, hugging her well-built form. Romy had slicked back her dark hair, making her look like a butch movie star, ready for the Academy Awards. Emerald quietly swooned in her velvet chaise, bringing the martini glass close to her lips.

"My, you look positively *dashing!*" Emerald cooed, standing to greet Romy. Stepping towards Romy, she couldn't resist the urge to finger the lapels of the tuxedo jacket, testing her limits of how close she could get to Romy. And to her surprise, Romy allowed her. "This is a gorgeous suit; it fits you *so* well. Where did you get it?"

Romy gave Emerald a cocky grin and replied, "I've had it for years. Working with high-profile clients, I sometimes need to dress up to fit in. Besides, I never know when a beautiful actress will invite me to a fancy opera, so it's good to be prepared."

Romy slyly winked, and Emerald nearly fainted. *Oh my god! Is Romy flirting with me? I must be having some kind of effect, after all!*

Suddenly, Emerald received a message on her phone that her driver was ready and waiting outside. Signaling Romy to follow, she lightly kissed Marilyn on the cheek. "Goodnight; we will see you in the morning."

"Night, dear. Oh, and please be careful," Marilyn said, a look of concern in her eyes. Picking up on the housekeeper's expression, Romy said reassuringly, "Don't worry; she is in good hands."

I'll bet I am! Emerald thought to herself as the women exited the mansion and traveled toward their respective vehicles.

Emerald and Romy were seated in the plush seats of her private VIP section of the Amelia Caruso Opera House within an hour. The curtains had lifted as the women became surrounded by the symphonious music and sumptuous stage decor. Emerald stirred in her seat, unable to concentrate amidst the alluring atmosphere. The warm scent of Romy's cologne permeated through Emerald like an aphrodisiac, and her pussy tingled with arousal.

Suddenly Emerald had a scandalous thought that couldn't be ignored. She craved to be pleasured by her handsome bodyguard. She could sense Romy's walls breaking down and knowing that they would be hidden in their private box, she placed a hand on Romy's dress pants and leaned in with a soft whisper, "Hey, I'm *really* horny for you. I'm not wearing any panties under my dress. I want you to go down on me here. Right now. In this box."

Emerald's eyes traveled to watch Romy's expression, which was a combination of confusion and slight alarm. Romy turned her face to whisper back, "What? Here? What do you mean?" Romy turned her head to look around the aisle. "There is staff here who could catch us!"

She was smirking as she traced her fingertips lightly over Romy's hand. "I know! Isn't that exciting? The thought of you between my legs, surrounded by the beauty of the opera, is making me so wet." Emerald became even more daring, touching the tip of Romy's earlobe and giving it a tiny lick. Then, purring, she added, "Don't worry. You know we have further security just outside our door whose main job is to make sure nobody comes in."

Romy shifted in her seat and bit her lip. Emerald could tell that Romy was turned on by the idea, even though she tried to remain professional. Emerald was determined to entice her; Romy seemed almost convinced. "I promise we won't get caught. Wait, I'll give you a sample, so you can taste what I'm offering."

Through the slit, Emerald slid her hand up her

gown towards her pubic bone. Reaching below, she touched her vulva, gathering her wetness on her fingertips. Then, she whispered insistently, "Open your mouth. I'm your client, and I am paying you to serve me. That means in *every way possible*. Open."

Emerald wasn't sure how Romy would respond and it looked for a moment like Romy would turn her down. Her fingers were centimetres from Romy's lips. She waited. Seconds later, Romy's mouth opened slightly and Emerald pushed her fingers lightly inside. Romy sucked on the finger and hummed.

This was having exactly the effect that Emerald had desired. The line between professional and personal had been crossed now.

"Get on your knees for me," she leant and whispered in Romy's ear.

She parted her legs and waited, leaning back even further in her velvet-lined chair as a hesitant, yet intrigued-looking Romy looked around carefully one last time before slowly lowering herself to her knees. It greatly aroused Emerald to have her strapping, powerful butch in a submissive position, looking up at her, with approval. "How's this? Can anyone see me?" Romy whispered as Emerald smiled, shaking her head no.

As much as Emerald enjoyed being more dominant, she also craved when someone could assume control of her body. For Emerald, the test of a good lover was a woman who could read the nuances of her desire and respond to the language of her movements. So rather than provide Romy with instructions on how she wanted to be plea- sured, she tried to sit back and allow Romy to work her own magic. "I feel like you'd know exactly what to do with me." Then, giving her bodyguard a wink, Emerald added, "Let's see if I'm right."

Emerald closed her eyes, feeling the hem of her gown rise with the touch of Romy's hands. As her palms glided up Emerald's thighs, she felt fingers deftly inch toward her pussy, which was already soaked with juices. Emerald could make out the shadow of Romy's head through the dark opera hall as it moved between her legs.

She placed her hands firmly on Romy, guiding her closer until she felt a flick of Romy's tongue on her clit. Slowly, her tongue traced around Emer- ald's clitoris and ran through her folds. Emerald moaned softly as her entire body relaxed against Romy's mouth. She pressed her pubic bone harder into Romy's mouth as the licks quickened with urgency. "Carry on like that and I'll come in your mouth," Emerald growled, almost forgetting they were in public.

Romy made a few muffled sounds as she continued to eat Emerald's pussy, switching between caressing movements of her tongue and focused suckling. The actress moved in tandem with Romy as her hips found a matching rhythm to Romy's mouth.

Intuitively, Romy looked up at Emerald, showing the actress her hand.

Emerald nodded vigorously. Romy's fingers were exactly what she needed right now. Her body was on fire, and there was no turning back. She *needed* to come.

She felt Romy's fingers pushing firmly inside of her and landing firmly at her G spot. She moaned, luckily drowned out by the music. The feeling building inside of her was delicious. Slowly, Romy's fingers moved in and out, hitting her G spot every time. It began to create waves of pleasure deep inside Emerald. Her eyes rolled back as Romy's mouth fixed back on her clitoris. Part of her couldn't believe that Romy had opened her mouth when she told her too and started all of this, and at the same time, Emerald couldn't imagine it any other way.

Emerald heard her own moans, trying to be mindful of her volume, but a more powerful force was building inside of her that would soon erupt like a volcano. Romy continued to stroke deep inside Emerald, quicker and harder. Finally, Emerald could feel an orgasm from within the depths of her body as pleasure overcame her.

The music surged within the hall as the stage came alive with symphonic cacophony. Every muscle within Emerald seized as a hot, white energy shot through her. Lost in ecstasy, she grabbed Romy's hair and held her head tightly as she rode out her orgasm.

While Emerald was still shaking from her climax, Romy slowly rose from the ground, slinking back in her seat. Emerald could feel her heart beating with a thrill that brought her life. Allowing her breath to return to normal, she sat quietly beside Romy and adjusted her dress.

As both women faced the stage, Emerald noticed Romy raise her fingers towards Emerald's face. Emerald turned to meet her gaze.

"I want you to taste yourself." Romy said quietly.

Emerald grinned, squealing on the inside. *Finally, I may have found a lover that can keep up with me!* She opened her mouth and sucked delicately on Romy's fingers tasting the sweet muskiness of her orgasm on Romy's strong fingers.

6

Romy stirred in her bed as her mind awoke before her eyes could open. Her subconscious mind drifted away as she returned to the present moment, which was the morning after the opera. Blinking, Romy shook her head against the pillow, still feeling the remnants of a dream she couldn't quite remember. But her memories of the night before were still fresh in her mind.

As she thought about eating Emerald out in the VIP box seats, her psyche was greeted with a surge of anxiety. Romy had a rule that she never became intimate with clients, regardless of how much they offered to pay her or how seductive they could be. And despite the many offers that she had received over her career, she had previously always been able to maintain her boundaries and professionalism. But last night tested the limits of Romy's discipline, and her strict self-control proved no match against the temptation of Emerald.

As soon as she had smelt the scent of Emerald's sex on her fingers, it had been all over for Romy.

Romy stretched out against the mattress, oscillating between guilt and excitement. She knew she had crossed a personal boundary but, at the same time, Emerald was a client who demanded whatever she desired. And if Romy was being honest with herself, it was a thrill to give into Emeralds' advances. Arousal stirred within Romy as she remembered the taste of Emerald's pussy and the delicate, earthy scent of the actress that lingered on Romy's fingers. *Fuck, she is incredibly intoxicating.*

As Romy faced the fact that she was attracted to Emerald, regret began to quiet in her mind as exhilaration overcame her consciousness. Romy had a sense that Emerald would continue such demands, and Romy knew she would concede, partly because Emerald made it clear that service was required of her. But also because Romy knew she wouldn't be able to resist. Emerald Crowle was an exceptional woman, and her sexual nature roused a hunger within Romy.

Hmmm, maybe we should discuss my contract in further detail. While I'm beginning to understand Emerald better, it's important that we get the particulars in writing. Romy thought to herself. *I can't have my reputation soiled by any undocumented missteps. Whenever Emerald wakes up, maybe we can chat about our arrangement so that it's clear.*

Romy rose from the mattress, stretching her arms above her head. She was about to throw on some clothes and make herself a coffee when suddenly, she heard the door chime, followed by a loud banging.

Considering Emerald's estate's isolation and the issues with the ex-husband, Romy immediately became alert. Grabbing a small hand pistol from her drawer, she shoved it into the back of her sweatpants and ran down the staircase to investigate the noise.

Again, the door chimed bellowed, and the thumping at the front door became deafening. Romy knew this was no ordinary house call; the energy coming from the outside was aggressive, and Romy had an idea of who the visitor may be.

As Romy reached the bottom of the stairs, Marilyn rushed towards her from the kitchen. "Oh my goodness, thank god you're here! I don't know who is causing so much noise at the door, but I was too frightened to open it."

"Don't worry; I'll deal with it. You're safe, head into the kitchen and stay there until I speak to whoever is at the door," Romy ordered Marilyn back to her station. Romy could make out a tall, menacing shadow as she approached the foyer. She tried to remain calm as her heart beat rapidly in her chest. No matter how many threatening situations Romy had been in, the sense of alarm never ceased. But the adrenaline was what kept her on her toes, giving her the mental and physical strength to confront this figure.

"Open the door, you bitch! Open this fucking door right now before I kick it in!" the figure bellowed from behind. Before Romy went to turn the knob, she slowly pulled her pistol from her pants, keeping it behind her back. Then, taking a deep breath, she opened the door, noticing the thick glass screen that served as a barrier between her and Thomas Black.

As soon as Thomas saw Romy, he shouted from the other side of the screen. "Where the hell is my ex-wife? Who the fuck are you? Answer me, bitch! Where is Emerald?"

His face was red and veiny, and the muscles under his shirt twitched with fury. Under other circumstances, the angry man would have frightened most people. But Romy was unfazed by his temper, citing it as an intimidation factor.

She was aware that Emerald's ex-husband was losing his temper because he had lost control of her. If he had ever truly had control of someone like Emerald in the first place. And in Romy's experience, no one was effective if they had no control over their emotions; she was confident in having the upper hand.

With one hand on her pistol, hiding it behind her, Romy calmly spoke from behind the screen. "Hello. I'm Ms. Crowle's new bodyguard. She does not want to speak to you or see you. You are no longer permitted on this property or anywhere close to Emerald."

Noticing their height was similar, Romy had no problem staring Thomas Black in the eyes as she spoke. I'll *bet his bark is bigger than his bite; I'm sure he's on steroids too.*

Romy continued, "If you approach the estate again, I will have you arrested for trespassing. Ms.

Crowle has filed a restraining order as well. So, you should be on your way." *Shit, I don't even know if Emerald filed—I hope so. If not, she needs to do that immediately.* Romy stood her ground as a barrier between her and Emerald.

Thomas's mouth curled into a snarky grin as his eyebrows furrowed. "Is that so? Well, let me tell you this, you fucking bulldog dyke. My ex-wife owes me money and half of this mansion. And if you think I'm not going to collect, you're crazy." Thomas took a few steps back from the door, pointing the finger at Romy. "You'll be seeing me again."

Then, turning his back, he spun around one last time. "Or maybe, you won't even see me coming." A sinister laugh escaped from Thomas as he left the path leading to the driveaway.

Shutting the heavy front door, Romy breathed a sigh of relief. But two things worried her; how Thomas could get past the estate gate and whether Emerald had filed a restraining order. Romy knew that she needed to troubleshoot these issues in addition to their contract.

From the corner of her eye, Romy saw Marilyn peeking out from behind the kitchen. Waving to her, she reassured the housekeeper that the coast was now clear. "It's okay; you can come out now. He's gone."

"Was that Thomas? Oh gosh, he is becoming scarier by the day. Thomas is ten times worse than he was when he and Emerald were married, and even then, he was a terror." Marilyn gulped, still looking fearful. "I'm worried about Ms. Crowle She's become so fragile since this drama began."

Romy felt terrible for Marilyn and Emerald, although it was hard to believe that Emerald was fragile. To Romy, she seemed as strong and seductive as she appeared in her films. And the threats from Thomas didn't seem to affect Emerald's sex drive. However, now that she had come face to face with the ex-husband, Romy better understood the potential danger facing the actress and her employees.

"What happened? Why was the doorbell going off?" Romy and Marilyn saw Emerald racing down the stairs, and Romy took a mental note of Emerald's see-through, black lace bodysuit that she tried to cover with a black, opaque robe. *My, my! Another sexy morning outfit. I don't know how she sleeps in that, but damn, she looks so fine.* Romy shook her head, trying to regain her focus, although Emerald had a delicious way of distracting her.

Looking at Emerald, Romy commanded, "You and I need to talk. We need to discuss some crucial elements with your home security. And we need to talk about our contract." Romy was fueled with adrenaline, and her patience was thin. As much as she enjoyed flirtatious banter with Emerald, the unexpected visit from Thomas threw Romy back into protective mode.

Emerald appeared surprised at Romy's tone but bobbed her head in agreement. The color in her face paled as she stated, "I guess it *was* Thomas at the door. Okay, let's talk." Emerald lowered her lean body into a chair in the dining hall, appearing as seductive as ever. It amazed Romy how the beautiful actress could simultaneously look so composed yet frightened. A strange emotion stirred within Romy, the desire to protect Emerald mixed with primal arousal. "Marilyn, could you make us some coffee, please?"

Romy sat across from Emerald, studying her features while Emerald lowered her eyes. *I think she finally understands the severity of this situation. I hope she listens to my advice.* A few moments later, Marilyn returned with two mugs filled with freshly brewed coffee. Emerald wrapped her hands around her cup as her lovely hazel eyes rose to meet Romy's. "Where should we start?"

Romy inhaled, feeling herself beginning to relax after this morning's chaos. "Well, first, you need stronger gate security. Who operates your system? I'm asking because somehow, Thomas was able to get to your front door, to ring the bell. If he can get that close, there's no telling what he will do."

Sighing, Emerald shrugged. "Marilyn takes care of that. It's a private, offsite system. I'm not really sure how it works, but I can ask her to speak to the company and make some adjustments." Romy nodded, "Yes, please do that immediately. And there is another thing. Have you filed a restraining order against your ex-husband? I'm here to protect you, but you can avoid a repeat of this morning with a restraining order."

"I spoke to my lawyer about it. He also suggested that, but I didn't know it would get this bad. Besides, I didn't want the media attention either." Emerald ran her hands through her golden-blond locks and arched her back into a stretch. "If I get a restraining order, will it remain private? I don't want people to know my situation."

Romy shrugged. "Well, I'm not going to tell

anyone. But you absolutely *need* to do this, Emerald. I'm serious. Would you like me to come with you to the police station? Would that make it easier?"

Emerald looked at Romy, grinning coyly. "You would do that for me? Oh, yes, I would love it if you came with me." She pressed her lips suggestively and added, "You're supposed to come with me *everywhere, anyway*, right?" She reached her hand across the table to touch Romy's elbow.

Romy bit her lip; Emeralds' charm was intoxicating. But Romy knew she needed to stay focused as there was more for the women to discuss. Clearing her throat, Romy responded. "Yeah, so about last night. I never sleep with my clients; yesterday was the first time that ever happened."

Then, touching Emerald's hand, which remained on Romy, she continued, "My first concern will always be your safety, and my second concern is *my* safety. My career means everything to me, and I will never put myself in a position where I can't be effective in my role."

Emerald's hazel eyes narrowed, becoming brighter. "I would never expect or desire you to be an ineffective bodyguard. What good would that be to me? I assume you will do the best job possible; you're certainly built for the position." Emerald's eyes examined Romy's frame. "But in dealing with me, there will be some *extra* requests. And you are expected to concede to my wishes."

Intrigued, Romy leaned in. "Oh yeah, like what?" Romy locked eyes with the actress, challenging her to share her desires. "Like, similar to last night?"

"Hmmm, mmm. Exactly. I expect you to service me however I wish. I want you to keep me safe, and I want you to make me come, whenever I want. I think I'm being pretty clear, yes?" The actress stared back at Romy as the corner of her mouth curved into a smile. "Why? Did you need that in writing?"

Romy's eyes widened. *Is it possible that this illustrious creature could also read minds?* Nodding, she agreed. "Yes, in fact, I do. Nothing explicit, of course. But a blanket statement, just to cover my ass."

Emerald winked. "Not a problem. In my line of work, contracts are as common as sexting. I'll speak to my personal assistant later today to make the arrangements. I can have a new contract created by the end of the day." Emerald leaned back into her chair and toyed with the straps of her lace bodysuit. "Is that all you wanted to discuss with me, *Romy?* Because if so, I have something I need to discuss with *you.*"

Romy shook her head and chuckled as Marilyn entered the dining hall to retrieve the coffee mugs. "Yeah, that's it. Oh, and a reminder to get a restraining order. Your turn."

"Would anyone like anything to eat?" the housekeeper asked, coming between the women. Emerald looked up at Marilyn and cheerily replied, "Not right now. Romy, did you want anything?" As Romy shook her head no, Emerald waved Marilyn away and added, "Okay, perfect. Because I'd like you to fuck me on top of my baby grand piano in the front living room."

Shocked, Romy gasped. She knew Emerald enjoyed flirting with her, but Romy wasn't expecting such an abrupt statement. Then, wide-eyed, she asked, "What?"

Emerald grinned. "You heard me. We are safe here. I'm horny for you; last night was only a tease, and I want *more.*" Emerald' 's lack of couth and her direct nature was a surprising turn-on, and suddenly, Romy became excited. Unfortunately, it was as if her brain was pulling her in two different directions, and Romy was succumbing to temptation.

"Let's go." Romy wanted to match Emerald's bold energy. But instead, Emerald stood to meet her, grabbing her hand as she led Romy out of the dining hall, turning right at the front foyer.

The formal living room was bright and airy, especially as the morning sun shone through the large bay windows. Directly in front of the pane was a large, shiny black piano. The cover was down, providing a flat surface. Emerald glided over, propping her body on top of the piano's exterior. Then, turning her head to the left, she met the windows and said, "I don't bother with curtains; they just get in the way. I've always fantasized about being fucked here while the sun shone on me." Looking around, Emerald added, "I doubt anyone will see us, but you never know. For me, it's part of the thrill!"

Romy shook her head in disbelief; Emerald was as outrageous as she was irresistible. Romy did not want to get caught, although she had to admit that the scene was thrilling. Slowly approaching Emerald, Romy ordered quietly, "Alright, open your legs for me."

Emerald slipped off her black robe and leaned

back, posing for Romy. "No. I want you to remove my bodysuit and slip it off my body first." Romy chuckled. "Of course, that's what you want. The helpless actress needs some attention, right?"

Doe-eyed, Emerald nodded, tracing her lips with her tongue. "That's right. And you're gonna give it to me. So don't act like you don't want to."

Wordlessly, Romy got closer until she was standing between Emerald's legs. As Emerald wrapped her thighs around Romy, Romy slowly slid down a strap of the lacy bodysuit, pausing to kiss Emerald's shoulder. Emerald smelt vaguely of her usual perfume, plus a faint trace of last night's sex. Her hair was tousled and she clearly hadn't showered and the thought of tasting her again nearly blew Romy's mind.

As her mouth traveled up Emerald's neck, Romy slipped the other strap down, exposing Emerald's breasts. They were surgically enhanced and well done. Her breasts were shaped like perfect teardrops and felt soft to the touch. As though Emerald could read her mind, she commented, "Saline. It's much softer than silicone. And my nipples are still *very* sensitive."

Romy took that as her cue to suck each rose-colored nipple, making them taut with her mouth.

Her hands traveled down the material, seeking Emerald's pussy. Emerald wrapped her hands around Romy, pulling her tight as she whispered in Romy's ear, "The bodysuit has snaps. You can rip it open."

Instantly, that information made Romy wet with arousal; she couldn't wait to undress Emerald and fuck her. Feeling for the snaps, Romy pulled at the center of the lingerie until the material parted, exposing Emerald's vulva and luscious lips. Romy dragged her fingers across Emerald's lips, then lifted them to Emerald's mouth, ordering, "Open your mouth and suck."

Emerald obeyed at once and Romy pushed three fingers inside her mouth as the actress ran her tongue around them before strongly sucking. Romy pulled out her fingers and glided them back in between Emerald's legs. She whispered, "This time, I'm using my fingers. But next time, you're getting my cock. You just need to learn to be patient first."

Before Emerald could say anything, Romy plunged three fingers deep inside her, feeling the spongy wetness and instinctively curling upwards to find her G spot. Emerald gasped. Her moans were loud and immediate and hellishly sexy. "Oh god, oh yeah! Just like that!" Romy began to thrust, gentle at first, but as Emerald's body reacted favorably, Romy quickened her pace, curling her fingers to stimulate the nerves of Emerald's g-spot. Emerald wrapped her legs harder around Romy, humping against Romy's hand.

As Emerald's vaginal muscles tightened around Romy's fingers, she knew Emerald was close to orgasm. "Yeah, come for me, baby. Is that what you want? You want to cum in front of the window while everyone watches you getting fucked by me?"

As Romy playfully taunted Emerald, she bucked hard, suddenly seizing in pleasure. "Oh fuck! Fuck yes..." Emerald roared in ecstasy, and the sounds of her satisfaction echoed through the large room. Her body was luscious as her back arched and her breasts rose, her head and golden hair tipped back. Romy couldn't help but think that the neighbors must have heard. Emerald was *loud*.

Emerald lay still for a few moments, catching her breath while Romy snuck a taste of Emerald's juices, popping a finger into her mouth. "God, you taste so good. I want more of you." Then, intoxicated by Emerald's essence, Romy turned to face her. Emerald was still sprawled on her back. "Open your legs for me."

"I usually don't take orders, but I am impressed by your appetite." Emerald parted her lean thighs as Romy moved her body to position her face in front of Emerald's glistening vulva. "Help yourself!"

Romy extended her tongue, seeking out Emerald's clitoris. Wrapping her lips around it, she began to lick gently. As her mouth switched from caressing to sucking Emerald's pussy, she could feel Emerald responding favorably, arching her back and moaning in pleasure. Ravenous, Romy felt an insatiable urge as she continued to devour Emerald. "I'm going to make you come again," Romy murmured, pausing what she was doing to take in how beautiful Emerald looked in rapture. "Lie back and give in to me."

Emerald parted her legs further as though welcoming Romy further in.

Romy quickened the pace of her tongue as Emerald's legs began to shake. Romy could feel her whole body beginning to shake as she held on to Emerald's hips. Then, bucking hard, Emerald cried out and ground her pussy against Romy's face, "Oh god, oh god, Romy! Fuck yes!" She pulled

Romy's hair so hard and gushed in her mouth. Romy devoured every drop she could and felt the remainder running down her chin.

Fuck, this woman is so hot.

Emerald gasped with pleasure before bursting into laughter. "Oh, I'm so sorry! I didn't realize I was hurting you." As Emerald relaxed again on the piano's surface, she gazed at Romy. "You know exactly how to fuck me and I like it."

Romy grinned wordlessly. She was aware that she could make women happy with her hands and her mouth. But it had been a long while since there had been a woman and certainly longer since there had been one that she wanted this much.

The movie star Emerald Crowle would be the one to seduce her- who would have imagined it?

The women were quiet, enjoying the silence, when Romy looked over the other side of the room. There was a small table covered with a white linen sheet. On the table where two plates, a butter dish, and a basket of pastries. Turning to Emerald, Romy asked, confused, "Is that *food* over there? Was that there from before?"

Emerald sat up, still on the piano's surface. "Oh, Marilyn must have put that out. She knows

7

"Marilyn? Can you please let Jesse know that we'll be a few minutes late? I'm taking a quick shower, and I need to get ready." Emerald had planned an outing to check out a property in Malibu. Ever since she had separated from Thomas, she had been interested in purchasing a third home, but the threats and drama had distracted Emerald from her search. But today, Emerald was looking forward to finally meeting with her real estate agent, and she felt more secure knowing that Romy would be by her side.

Emerald hummed to herself as she opened her closet, indecisive about what to wear. Her body was still buzzing from the morning's orgasmic bliss, and her attraction to Romy was strong. Emerald always felt her best whenever she procured a lover; enjoying amazing sex with women gave Emerald's life validity and meaning. But there was something extraordinary about her new bodyguard that made Emerald's head spin with desire.

Her spirit felt renewed and playful; Emerald planned to keep her arrangement with Romy hot and fresh. Aware of her seductive powers, Emerald sauntered down the hall in a red lace bra and matching panties. She stood in front of Romy's door and knocked.

"Hello? Romy?" Emerald posed against the doorframe, ready to impress Romy in her lingerie. It gave the actress a thrill to tease her; no matter how aloof Romy appeared, Emerald was aware that Romy was also attracted to her.

The door opened, and Romy's expression went from neutral to surprised. "Um, hi! Is that what you're wearing today?" Romy smirked as her eyes traveled downwards, sending a thrill through Emerald. She could tell that Romy was enjoying the show.

"Well, actually, I wanted to ask if you could

help me pick out an outfit. I want to look my best for this appointment, and I'd *love* a second opinion." Emerald batted her lashes as she suggestively ran her fingers over her lace-clad breasts.

Romy chuckled, running a hand through her short, dark hair. Dimples formed on her cheek as she replied, "Sure, but I'm no expert on feminine styles. Don't you think Marilyn would be a better help?"

Emerald playfully pouted. "I guess you're right. But maybe you can help me undress when we get home."

"That sounds like a better job for me, especially if my role includes servicing you in every way possible," Romy quipped, raising an eyebrow. Emerald loved how she could bring out a naughty side in Romy; it was deliciously arousing.

"You're a fast learner; I like that." Emerald winked. "Okay, I'll leave you to get ready. Please meet me downstairs by the front entrance. My driver is coming soon, and you'll be driving right behind us."

"Sounds good, boss." Romy grinned, giving Emerald a once-over before closing the door. Emerald padded back to her bedroom, enjoying her flirtatious banter with Romy. Emerald joined

Romy downstairs within thirty minutes, noticing the black SUV parked directly in front of the entrance.

"That's Jesse; I'm getting in. I'll see you at the address." Emerald turned to wave at Romy. Romy replied, "Alright, I'm getting in my vehicle now. I'll be directly behind you."

Emerald smiled as she stepped outside. The sky was clear blue, and the sun shone brightly. *Ah, the perfect day to see the house of my dreams. All the bad energy of the past few weeks is finally dissipating, and now, I can enjoy some peace. And it's lovely having Romy around. She knows exactly how to brighten my spirits.*

"Good morning, Jesse!" Emerald exclaimed as she slid into the back of the luxury vehicle. "How are you?"

"Very well, Ms. Crowle. We're driving to Malibu, correct?" the driver asked as Emerald responded, "Yes, that's right. We are going to 685 Oceanview Heights. Romy will be driving immediately behind us to keep an eye on things."

Emerald saw the driver nodding as he kept his eyes on the road. "Sure, ma'am, no problem. I'll be sure to get you there safely." Emerald leaned back against the plush leather interior, sliding on a pair of Chanel sunglasses. As Emerald relaxed in the vehicle, she entertained memories of Romy fucking her.

Emerald could still feel Romy's thick fingers plunging deep inside her as her hot tongue teased and sucked on her clit. The thought of Romy's muscular physique and handsome features aroused Emerald as she thought, *Mmmm, if the drive were any longer, I'd pleasure myself right here!*

She continued to let her mind wander when suddenly, the car swerved abruptly. As the tires screeched, Emerald came to full attention, grabbing the front seat. She exclaimed, "Jesse! What happened?"

"Hold on, Ms. Crowle. There seems to be a crazy driver on the road right in front of us. The car keeps veering side to side." Jesse Stone looked back at Emerald reassuringly. "Don't worry; I'm trying to pass the vehicle. Just stay calm; I've got this under control."

But Emerald's heart sank, sensing that there could be more to this situation.

She peered over the front seat to get a better look at the car. Emerald noticed the vehicle was a red Porsche, which relieved her since she didn't know anyone who drove that model. *That can't be*

Thomas; he drives a white Thunderbird. Emerald gripped her seatbelt while trying her best to stay cool when the black SUV unexpectedly halted, lurching her body forward.

"Ah, Jesse! What's happening?" Emerald panicked as Jesse turned to face the actress. "I'm not sure, Ms., but I'm calling 911 right now." From the front window, Emerald saw that the red Porsche had completely blocked her SUV, leaving her and Jesse stuck on the road. But just as Jesse pulled out his phone to call for help, three men got out of the Porsche, one of whom was Thomas.

"Oh my god! It's Thomas, and he's not alone!" Emerald turned around, relieved to see Romy parked behind her. She waved furiously at the guard to get Romy's attention. The bodyguard was motioning at Emerald to stay in her car, but Emerald's emotions were heightened. Against her better judgment, Emerald escaped from the backseat and ran towards Thomas, her arms flailing in distress.

"What the fuck are you doing? You psycho! You trapped us on the road!" A violent fury surged through Emerald as she lashed out at her ex-husband. "You're going to be sorry you messed with me!"

The two unrecognizable men stood on either

side of Thomas as he squared off with Emerald. "You're the sorry one, bitch. You are just an old, washed-up actress who likes to eat men up and spit them out." Thomas was built like a brick out house, and while his height was comparable to Emerald's, he was strong enough to snap her like a twig. "If you want to pass us on the road, you'll have to pay up. And I mean, right now." Thomas's associates sneered at Emerald, laughing like threatening hyenas.

Emerald's eyes widened; she was caught between anger and fear. She was never one to back down from a fight, but even Emerald knew her dangerous situation.

One of the men swiftly blocked the front door of the SUV, obstructing Jesse from escaping the vehicle. Then, another man moved quickly behind Emerald as Thomas lurched in front of her.

But just as Thomas attempted to grab Emerald, Romy suddenly appeared behind him. Caught up in the chaos of the moment, Emerald didn't even notice Romy sneak up on the group. But within seconds, Romy caused Thomas to tumble to the ground with a sharp jab to the back of his kneecap. As he was caught off-guard, heclumsily fell just as Emerald scurried out of the way.

Romy threw her elbow, blocking an incoming punch from the guy standing behind Emerald.

Before the thug could attack Romy again, she punched him squarely in the gut, causing the man to keel over and vomit. Emerald stood back, her jaw agape. She was shocked by the deftness of Romy's defense. As Thomas attempted to grab Romy, she swiftly turned her body, smacking him against the head with a strong roundhouse kick.

The third attacker, who had blocked in the driver, looked skittishly at the scene. Both Thomas and the other male were flailing on the ground. He nervously walked back towards the red Porsche, throwing his hands up in the air. "You crazy bitches! I'm fucking out of here, man."

Adrenaline surged through Emerald; she couldn't believe how Romy handled the attackers. Even in the movie industry for countless decades, Emerald had never seen a woman defend herself with such agility and swiftness.

Glancing at Thomas, who lay coughing, face down in the dirt. Emerald shouted, "Ah-ha! See? I told you; you'd be sorry for messing with me! You're a worthless, disgusting man—I never loved you!" Stomping towards her ex-husband, Emerald poised her foot to kick him in the ribs. "You're nothing but a pathetic, wanna-be celebrity. You'll never get a cent from me!" Just as Emerald was about to attack, she felt a firm grip around her waist.

"Emerald, we need to go now!" Romy had wrapped her arms tightly against the actress, yanking her away from Thomas and his associate, both of whom remained injured on the ground. The bodyguard shouted at Jesse, signaling him to drive away from the scene. Emerald succumbed to Romy's grasp, allowing herself to be taken away into Romy's vehicle.

"Get in the passenger seat and stay put!" Romy ordered Emerald to remain in the car while she hit the gas, fleeing from the incident. Emerald clung to the dashboard while Romy sped away until the vehicle was far from where Thomas and his acquaintance had been left. Slowly, Emerald began to relax, and she snuck a peek at Romy, whose eyes were fixed on the road. Her senses were heightened, and the starlet felt a rush through her body that she had never experienced.

Coyly, she began, "That was *very* impressive. I had no idea how skilled you were at martial arts." Emerald lightly touched Romy's arm, squeezing her firm bicep. "Thank you for protecting me."

Romy remained focused on her driving, glancing at Emerald. "You're welcome; it's my job. I had no idea that you had such a feisty temper. But Thomas and his thugs are no joke; you can't antagonize those guys like that." Romy frowned and shook her head.

Licking her lips suggestively, Emerald replied, "I know, you're right. Sometimes, my temper can go too far. But I'm not a weak person either, and I've learned to stand up for myself when I need to." Emerald moved her hand from Romy's bicep to the top of her thigh, slightly parting her legs.

To Emerald's delight, Romy took a hand from the steering wheel and placed it on Emerald's leg. Her body was humming with desire, and despite Romy's chastising, she could sense attraction from the bodyguard. Her panties began to moisten as she looked at Romy again. Then, overcome with an urge for sex, Emerald asked seductively, "Can we pull over on the side of the road? I want you so bad; I need you inside me again."

Romy tried to remain serious, but Emerald noticed her dimple appearing as Romy hid her smile. She knew that Romy wanted her, too. Running her fingers up Romy's thigh, she leaned in closer, teasing Romy with her breath. "Come *on*;

I know you want to. Seeing you kick those guys' asses made me *so* horny."

Romy turned to face Emerald and grinned. "Whatever the princess wants, the princess gets, huh?" Romy looked ahead, spotting a side road. Pulling off to the side, and pulling in behind a tree-line, Romy looked carefully around as though to assess their safety, and upon seemingly deciding it was safe, Romy turned off the ignition and faced Emerald. "I love how badly you want me. Tell me again, *slowly*."

Emerald's mouth curled into a smile as she unbuckled her seatbelt. Then, hiking up her skirt, Emerald turned herself forward. She maintained eye contact, leaning closer. Then, moving her gaze to Romy's mouth, Emerald whispered, "I. Want. You. Right. Now."

"Get on top of me," Romy directed as she removed her seatbelt, sliding the car seat back slightly. Emerald straddled her, feeling Romy's hand against her underwear. Romy's fingers began to massage her vulva, rubbing her clit through her underwear. Emerald ground her pussy against Romy's hand, craving deep penetration. She moved her hips slowly, savoring the delicious sensation of friction. "Should I take these off?"

"No, I'm just going to move them to the side to give you a quick and dirty fuck," Romy replied in a thick, throaty voice, and her primal expression ignited a powerful desire within Emerald. To her, Romy had always come across as stoic, almost detached, but in that moment, Romy's passionate nature shone through, driving Emerald crazy.

Romy deftly moved the material, plunging her fingers deep inside Emerald's wetness. Her body seized with pleasure upon the first thrust, and as Romy began to fuck her, Emerald felt her soul leave her body in ecstasy. She bounced up and down on Romy's hand, wanting harder and faster thrusts.

As she moaned and sighed, the car windows began to fog. "Do you like that, you slutty little diva? I want you to take it, take my fingers deep in your hot, little pussy."

"Oh fuck, you know I do! I *love* how you fuck me. Please, yes, just like that!" Emerald exclaimed, arching her back. Romy continued to finger fuck Emerald until she felt herself climax.

"Oh fuck, yes, yes, yes!" Emerald came hard, throwing her head back and squeezing Romy's body.

The women lay together for a few minutes as

Emerald caught her breath. "Jesus, you are amazing! You know how to fuck, and you know how to fight; what can't you do?"

Emerald lifted herself off of Romy finally and felt her juices running down her inner thigh.

She felt in a daze from the fucking.

Romy put her aviators back on and looked over at Emerald as she restarted the engine.

"Where to, Ma'am?"

Her hair was slightly mussed from the sex and her bare skin glowed in the sunlight. Emerald had never felt more attracted to anyone in her whole life.

8

Romy waited until Emerald finished her call. After they stopped briefly to play, Emerald decided to cancel the Malibu home viewing. She stated she was too overwhelmed by the day's events to focus on real estate.

"Hi Gloria, yes, it's Emerald Crowle calling. I'm so sorry to do this on such short notice, but could we move the viewing to another day? I've had a terrible headache all morning, and I'm afraid I won't be able to make it." Romy watched Emerald as she fabricated her excuse. But she couldn't blame Emerald for lying; she knew how tough living in the public eye must be. If word got out about the attack from Thomas, the paparazzi would never leave her alone.

"Oh, good. Perfect, thank you so much," Emerald purred, satisfied with the news. "I'll see you then." Hanging up, Emerald grinned at Romy. "I can go back next Friday. Now, let's head to Rodeo; I need some retail therapy to calm my nerves."

Romy raised her eyebrows, teasing her, "That massive orgasm wasn't enough to relax you? Shit, maybe I'm losing my touch." Emerald playfully laughed. "Oh, I can assure you; you have an amazing touch. But I'm a woman with many needs, one of which is a new gown to wear during awards season."

"Alright, let's go." Romy navigated the vehicle back onto the freeway and tried to keep her attention on her driving. But her mind was swirling with a range of emotions, attraction, adrenaline, and confusion. Emerald's advances were irresistible. Romy found herself caught between wanting to remain aloof and being drawn in by Emerald's magnetic charm. Romy had never been in a position where she allowed a client's behavior to affect her focus.

Emerald's bold flirtations, combined with

unpredictable and dangerous elements, were causing Romy's stoicism to crumble. And she knew that her entanglement with Emerald would complicate their working relationship. And yet, there was a force drawing Romy deeper into Emerald's life, and she felt like she was sinking into a quicksand of drama and lust.

As she brushed a hand through her hand, she caught a whiff of Emeralds' intoxicating scent on her fingers. Romy bit her lip and inhaled; the earthy fragrance stirred a primal desire within her.

Her mouth watered with an insatiable hunger as Emerald commented, "When we get to Rodeo, I'd like to visit Jessica Lyon's; it's my favorite dress shop on the strip and *very* exclusive. In fact, the owner will ensure my privacy, closing off the entire store for me."

Emerald looked at Romy as though she expected her to be impressed. Emerald inched her fingers across Romy's thigh, teasing her. "We might even get the whole place to ourselves, including the *dressing room.* That could be fun, yes?"

"No problem, just give me the directions, and I'll get us there quickly." Romy wanted to concede to Emerald's suggestive behavior, but between the attempted-carjacking incident and the spontaneous sex in the car, Romy's mind was overstimulated. Most of all, she was concerned for Emerald's safety. Romy thought to herself, *It's as if she had forgotten why she hired me in the first place. And she doesn't even seem affected by today's events. Maybe she's just an incredible actress, and I can't tell.*

Turning quickly to look at Emerald, Romy stated, "Listen, I've been enjoying these intermittent affairs with you as a part of my job. But I'm worried about Thomas. I'm capable enough to defend you—as well as myself—but, considering that he runs with a violent crew, I can't predict what he is capable of, and I want you to also be on guard."

Emerald remained silent for a few minutes as the car turned onto Rodeo Drive. Massive palm trees lined the street, which was decorated with high-end, designer stores. Given that Romy had worked with other high-end clients, she was familiar with the area and knew it was far safer for Emerald to be here than somewhere on the open road. Once the vehicle stopped in front of Jessica Lyon's, Emerald unbuckled her seat belt and looked at Romy.

"I understand what you're saying, and I don't want to make this job harder for you. I've always been independent, and I've refused to live in fear for most of my life." Romy was surprised by the assertion in Emerald's tone, which had been mostly soft and flirtatious. "This is the first time in 58 years that I feel a sense of danger. But I don't want that to affect how I live my life or my sense of freedom. So I'll follow your advice, Romy. But please don't treat me like a child. Is that clear?"

Romy's heart sank. She didn't mean to insult Emerald, who was also her paying client. Touching her hand, Romy replied, "Yes, it's clear. And I'm sorry if I came off condescending. I know that you are a strong and brave woman. I care about you, and I want to do an effective job. That's all."

Emerald's expression softened as her mouth curved into a coy smile. "Thanks, Romy. To be honest, I'm *also* worried. But right now, I want to try on some dresses and forget about this morning." She squeezed Romy's hand before both women exited the car, with Emerald leading her into the store.

"Emerald! Oh my goodness, it's been *ages!*" A mature-looking woman with short, white-blond hair, dressed in a stylish pantsuit, embraced Emerald as she entered the large, airy dress shop.

"Oh, Jessica, I was hoping to see you!" Emerald

and the store owner air kissed as Romy hung back. She often felt out of place amidst artificial greetings, and Romy wasn't as gregarious as her client. "I'm looking for a gown for an upcoming awards show. I'm wondering if I could take some time and shop in private?"

Jessica grinned, winking at Emerald. "Anything for you, my dear." Jessica nodded to the other shop assistant who promptly shut the front door and turned a *closed* sign to face the window. "It's lovely to see you. But, please, take all of the time you need."

"Oh, where are my manners? This is Romy Russell, an associate of mine." Emerald presented Romy as though she was an accessory, but Romy wasn't offended. It was Emerald's right to keep her personal affairs or hires private, especially for someone of her stature.

"Hello, nice to meet you. Please, have a seat." Jessica politely offered Romy a velvet-covered bench to sit on while Emerald perused the many racks that held expensive, sparking gowns. Romy took her place and waited patiently while Emerald flitted around like a hummingbird.

After two hours of trying on dresses and conversing with the shop owner, Emerald announced that she was ready to leave. "I'd like to leave the dress here until the adjustments are made. I'll be sending Marilyn to pick it up." Emerald held a long, white dress that appeared to be covered in Swarovski crystals. Jessica took the dress from Emerald, encasing it in a garment bag.

"Of course, my dear. The dress will be waiting for pickup. Thank you again for coming in." Jessica and Emerald embraced again before she and Romy left the shop.

"Do you feel better?" Romy asked. "Yes, I love the dress, it is perfect, and I definitely feel better. Thanks for taking me here." Emerald put an arm around the small of Romy's back. "Now, I'd like to visit Myers Jewelry because I'll need a necklace to go with the dress. It's just a few blocks south."

Romy nodded. "Sure, but I'd like to stop by the car first. I left my water bottle in the front seat." Romy and Emerald crossed the street towards Romy's vehicle when suddenly, two men appeared from around the corner. Instantly, Romy recognized them as associates of Thomas Black. When the men saw Romy and Emerald, they drew their guns.

Romy moved quickly to block Emerald, pulling out her pistol. *Pop!* One of the men shot his gun in the direction of the woman, and Romy yelled, "Get in the car, Emerald! Now, get in!" Emerald screamed and ducked, running to the passenger side. In her panic, her shaky fingers struggled to open the door handle. Romy shouted, trying to keep her eyes on the shooters while watching Emerald race into the car and staying between Emerald and the shooters.

Romy fired her pistol, moving deftly and with confidence. The other associate fired his gun once again before both men turned to escape in the other direction. Luckily neither Romy nor Emerald was injured, but the shots unnerved Romy. If she hadn't been with Emerald, Romy would have chased the men. But her priority was Emerald, and Romy wanted to leave the scene immediately to get Emerald back to her estate.

"Holy shit! Are you okay?" Romy asked breathlessly as Emerald keeled over and burst into tears. Romy, who was also shaking, wanted to appear strong. She wrapped her arms around the actress, allowing her to cry. Romy felt helpless as she patted Emerald's back, whispering, "It's okay, you're safe. I'm taking you home right now."

Emerald continued to sob as Romy navigated the vehicle away from Rodeo Drive and onto the

9

E merald awoke feeling groggy and depressed. Blinking her eyes, she looked at the clock on her nightstand. It read 4:45 am. A day following the shooting, Emerald spoke to her agent about taking a week off filming to deal with "personal matters." Luckily, Emerald being who she was, her requests were rarely denied.

Considering the events from the past few days, Emerald couldn't concentrate on her script, and until this issue with Thomas was solved, she was concerned that her work would suffer. Emerald was hoping to get more rest, but unfortunately, her body clock was primed to wake up early, even if she didn't have to be anywhere this morning.

As she rolled over, snuggling her pillow, remnants of a forgotten nightmare began to reappear in her consciousness. Emerald closed her eyes, trying to recall the details. She remembered a crowd surrounding her; it was a mixture of cold, angry faces combined with expressions of adoration. Emerald didn't recognize anyone in the group, but when a finger tapped her on the shoulder, she turned around to see Romy.

She was so excited to see the bodyguard, but when Emerald went to embrace Romy, the Romy's face turned mean, transforming Romy into Thomas. Then, Emerald felt a sense of intense fear. A gun went off amidst the crowd, and Emerald screamed. She sat up in bed as her subconscious mind subsided, leaving her alone and frightened in the dark.

"Fuck, maybe I'll take a bubble bath to relax me. It's too early to bother Marilyn with anything. Hopefully, this will help me fall asleep," Emerald said to herself, the sound of her voice filling the lonely, dark room. She rose from her bed, fully nude, and padded over to her ensuite bathroom. Pouring a bit of rose-scented soap into her large soaker tub, Emerald watched as the water flowed from the tap in a daze. *God, I'm still half asleep—I hope I don't drown!*

Once the tub was filled, Emerald lowered herself into the warm, soothing water. "Ahhh, yes, that's perfect." A delicate fragrance wafted from the porcelain bath, calming her nerves. But as Emerald sank deeper into the water, allowing her body to be fully immersed, she couldn't ignore the nagging feeling of anxiety that lay deep in the pit of her gut. She couldn't vocalize her feelings out loud, not even to Marilyn. But the truth was that Emerald was utterly shaken by the incidents of the days prior, and at this point, her insides felt alive with fear.

Whenever Emerald felt out of sorts, sex was her go-to remedy to calm and center herself. Knowing that she could seduce almost anyone was a delicious way to assuage her ego. Emerald knew that she could pay Romy a visit to have Romy pleasure her, but something was blocking her desire. So instead, Emerald decided to masturbate, which normally alleviated such undesirable emotions.

Parting her legs, Emerald reached her hand below the water to touch herself. Emerald tried to evoke pleasurable sensations with her fingers, but she was having difficulty feeling anything.

Licking her lips and closing her eyes, Emerald thought about Romy fucking her in the car on the side of the road. She remembered straddling the strong, butch bodyguard and how wet and aroused it made her. Usually, such fantasies would be enough to turn Emerald on; her mind wasn't connecting with her body. She knew how attracted she was to Romy, so the fact that, physically, she couldn't feel any favorable sensations alarmed her. *What is wrong with me? Why isn't this working?*

The more she tried to pleasure herself using different hand techniques, the more frustrated Emerald became. Finally, she gave up and slumped into the tub, feeling the water starting to cool. Another emotion bubbled from her core, one of intense loneliness and despair. As soon as it hit Emerald, she began to cry, lifting her knees to her chest; it was not the release Emerald desired. But once the tears started falling, this dam of emotion burst open.

Emerald had to admit defeat; there was no escaping or pretending at this moment. *Well, at least I'm alone. I wouldn't want anyone to see me looking so pathetic.*

Emerald allowed herself to grieve the darker parts of her life that were left out of her public persona. While Emerald didn't often dwell on her hidden sexual orientation, the fact that her existence felt fraudulent hurt her soul. Deep down, Emerald was aware that she had been acting throughout her entire life and not just on set. And those concealed desires were the primary source of her loneliness.

Suppressing a significant part of herself had also caused Emerald to behave in opportunistic and egotistical ways, often preventing others from becoming close to her. Fans were not the same as friends, but Emerald did her best to maintain connections that were dependent on her for their livelihood. Splashing some water on her face, she murmured to herself, "Hmmm, maybe that's why I'm so drawn to Romy. She doesn't seem to need anyone, which scares me a little. I don't want her to go."

After rising from the bath, Emerald decided to go back to her room to get more sleep. But, as she snuggled under her down duvet, a thought came to her. *I should ask Romy if she wants to spend some real, quality time with me tonight outside the context of her job. I'd really like to get to know her better. And I don't want her to think I'm some vain, superficial monster.*

Emerald couldn't place the time, but at some point, there was a knock as a voice behind the door called out, "Emerald? It's Romy. Are you still asleep?" Emerald rolled over and looked at the clock on her nightstand. *Oh my god, it's 3:45 pm!* With a start, she sat up. "Romy? I'm awake. Come in."

She shook her head, feeling disorientated. Romy slowly opened the door, peeking her head inside. "I'm sorry to disturb you. We were worried about you, and I wanted to see if you were okay."

Emerald grinned, and her heart burst with gratitude. Waving Romy into the room, Emerald rubbed her face, patting down her hair. "I don't know how I managed to sleep so late! I got up in the early morning for a bit and took a bath. I only meant to sleep for a few more hours." Emerald sat up, feeling alert. "I guess I needed the rest."

Romy sat on the edge of Emerald's bed, her eyes empathetic. "I'm sure you did. Yesterday was intense." She gently put a comforting hand on Emerald's shoulder. "Are you okay?"

The question struck a nerve within Emerald. It was rare for anyone to sincerely ask if she was okay. Emerald found herself softening inside, and she had this incredible urge to crawl into Romy's arms and cry. But Emerald was still proud and conceited, and she wasn't ready to allow anyone to see her vulnerabilities, especially not her hot, butch bodyguard.

"I'll be fine, thank you. But I thought I'd like to enjoy a cozy night in, and I wondered if you wanted to spend some time with me?" Emerald batted her lashes, turning on the charm. "I could use the company."

Romy nodded. "Sure, that sounds nice. I could use a break from the drama myself after yesterday. What did you have in mind?"

Emerald thought, her hazel eyes turning to the ceiling. "Oh, I know! I'll ask Marilyn to make a steak dinner, and we can enjoy our dinner on the patio in the garden. It's so lovely out there, especially with the tea lights."

"That sounds great! This afternoon, I was going to stop by the gun range for some practice, and then I want to take more time to investigate this case. I've sorted the gate and estate security- we should be safe at home now at least." Romy stood from the bed. "Unless you need anything else from me, I'll be back around 6:00 pm."

"That's perfect. I'll get my driver to hit Whole Foods, and then Marilyn will prepare our dinner. I'll see you then." Emerald locked eyes with Romy, feeling her stomach flutter. It had been a long time since she had made plans with someone without being related to a job or an opportunity.

With a rise in her spirits, Emerald got up and prepared herself for the evening ahead. Emerald always wanted to look her best, but she wanted to wear more relaxed attire tonight. After donning a long, flowy sundress that showed off her curves, Emerald sought out her hired help to inform them of tonight's plans.

Later in the evening found Emerald and Romy outside on the expansive property. The night air was thick with humidity, and the hum of crickets surrounded the women. After they had enjoyed a hearty steak dinner with plenty of red wine, Marilyn presented the women with Emerald's favorite cognac. The actress turned to clink her glass against Romy's, her face glowing by candle-light. "I *love* a delicious digestif after dinner, don't you?"

To Emerald's surprise, Romy nodded, replying, "I do. In fact, a past lover of mine was a rep for

Remy Martin." Romy took a breath from the sifter and smiled. "But this is a much better brand."

Emerald grinned. "That is so interesting! I actually know the CEO of Remy Martin; he was good friends with my second ex-husband. They used to go golfing at the Mulberry Country Club. And they also loved working out at the nearby fitness center across the street." Romy interjected, asking excitedly, "CrossTown Fitness? I used to work there as a trainer for two years. It was one of my jobs as I was working towards my security license. What a small world!"

The conversation effortlessly flowed as soon as their external connection had been established. Emerald was amazed to find out that there was much crossover between many of their mutual acquaintances. Gazing at Romy, her sparkling blue eyes and strong jawline, Emerald felt a deep sense of comfort and familiarity. "I'm surprised we hadn't met sooner. We have so much in common." Then, looking out into the courtyard, the actress suggested, "Would you like to stroll around the garden? The air is so lovely right now. I love a hot summer night!"

Romy agreed, and the women walked along the circumference of the grounds. Emerald had an irresistible urge to grab Romy's hand, but she didn't dare. While Emerald was well versed in the powers of sexual seduction, she had less experience relaxing with a woman as her true self. Some days, Emerald wasn't even sure who she truly was, but tonight, she felt the layers of walls melt away, and suddenly, Emerald felt new and innocent, even shy.

"So, what made you want to become an actress?" Romy asked. Soft gravel crunched under their feet as they made their way to the back entrance of the estate.

Emerald smiled, thinking back to her childhood. So many people had asked her that question, but Emerald always felt pressured to give a canned response in accordance with her public image. But with Romy, she thought that she could be honest.

"Well, when I was ten years old, our fifth-grade teacher, Ms. Barlow, also taught drama. It was nothing intense; we were just kids." Emerald shrugged before she continued, "But I loved transforming into someone different, becoming a character. With acting, I could be anyone I wanted, and it felt so freeing to me. But I, well, I also loved Ms. Barlow."

Emerald suddenly placed a hand on Romy's forearm. "That stays between us, okay? I've never told anyone that. But I think that was the first time I realized I was gay. Or at least that I was *different.* But acting afforded me the luxury of *being* different; it's where I fit in." Chuckling, she added, "But things changed when I came to Hollywood. Once the opportunities started to come, I was limited on how different I was allowed to be, and that complicated things. But the trade-off was success and fame, and god knows how hard I worked for that."

"It must be hard on you," Romy commented. "I couldn't imagine not being able to live authentically. I've been out for as long as I can remember. Shit, I think I came out of the womb as a full-fledged dyke!" The women shared a laugh as Romy continued, "But my life has also been unconventional, especially my career choice. Maybe it's because I've also felt different and sought comfort in unique spaces where I could thrive, as opposed to hiding."

Emerald nodded, taking in what Romy had said. She felt a bond of understanding growing between them, and it softened Emerald, making her feel connected. The conversation between them flowed effortlessly, she felt completely in the moment until the lights in the garden turned off.

Romy stopped in her tracks, appearing alert. But Emerald commented, "Don't worry, they are on an automatic timer. So, I'm guessing it must be midnight by now. I didn't even realize the time!"

"Do you want to head back inside?" Romy asked. "I'm getting a little tired. But, unlike you, I got up in the morning." Emerald playfully elbowed Romy while wishing the night didn't have to end.

"Sure, we can, but, um, I have a small request," Emerald propositioned. "I—well, I haven't been sleeping well. Not just because of the recent events but for a *while*." Taking a deep breath, she faced Romy. "Could you sleep in my room with me tonight? I'm not looking for sex. I just really need the company."

Romy's expression changed from guarded to gentle. Then, narrowing her eyes, she looked directly at Emerald and replied, "Sure, yes, I'm happy to do that."

"Okay, thank you." Emerald smiled, feeling herself glow from the inside. "I'll head up to my room and give you some time to prepare for bed. Just enter when you're ready; you don't need to knock."

The women traveled up the long, winding staircase with Emerald trailing behind. She was lost in her thoughts, feeling peaceful and dreamy from her evening with Romy. Once in her room, she took a quick shower and slid into a plain, black lace negligee. The lingerie was simple in comparison to other, more scandalous looks. But the gown was made of quality silk and comfortable for sleeping. Unlike most nights where she sought distraction, Emerald desired comfort and warmth tonight. And she was excited to share her bed with Romy.

Tucking herself under her duvet, Emerald waited in the quiet room until she heard the door creak open. "Hi," Romy whispered, slowly closing the door behind her. "I hope I didn't wake you."

Romy wore shorts and a tank top. She looked beautiful in the dim light.

"No, you're fine. Please, get in under the covers." Emerald felt the weight of Romy's body beside her, sinking into the mattress. She turned her back to Romy and asked, "Could you spoon me? I can't tell you how long it's been since I felt someone hold me in bed."

Romy agreed, wrapping her muscular arms around Emerald's petite frame. Immediately,

Emerald sighed, leaning into the warmth of Romy's hug. It felt like Emerald had just received a meal after years of starvation. Every muscle in her body relaxed as Romy's gentle breath tickled her neck. "Thank you. I feel so safe right now. You're the best bodyguard I've ever had." Emerald uttered, feeling sleepy.

Romy stroked Emerald's hair, fingering the delicate curls. "You are safe. I promised to protect you, and I will." Emerald purred inwardly, relishing in Romy's touch and soft caresses. Before long, Emerald fell deeply asleep, nestled in Romy's strong arms.

10

"Yup, coming!" Romy refilled their glasses with cold, filtered water. The women were lying in the sun at the back of the estate. She returned with the drinks, handing one to Emerald.

The past week was quiet at the mansion. While Romy enjoyed the peace, the nature of her job required constant focus, and she was having trouble relaxing. Emerald continued receiving frightening threats and aggressive text messages from Thomas, which Romy could tell affected her ability to socialize.

But neither he nor his lackeys showed up in person. Romy knew that Emerald was on edge, and she, too, remained at attention until the next shoe dropped, which Romy felt would be soon. Once they returned inside from suntanning, Romy was going to continue her investigation of Emerald's ex-husband to determine his next move.

"Oh, thank you!" Emerald took the glass from Romy. "It's so hot and lovely today; I think I'm going to sunbathe topless." Then, giving Romy a wink, she turned to ask suggestively, "Do you want to help me with the bikini strings? I could use some sunscreen, too, if you don't mind."

Romy chortled, rolling her eyes. But naturally, she didn't mind. Emerald was stunningly beautiful, and her body remained luscious and toned. And Romy was starting to realize that Emerald's flirtatious manner was her way of communicating; the teasing was never malicious in its intent. She began to see more authenticity and vulnerability in Emerald.

Romy still felt unsure about Emerald's motives but seeing a more genuine version of Emerald was reassuring. Romy began to warm up to her antics and often outrageous personality. "Sure, turn around. I'll get your back and shoulders."

"You're the best. And oh my god, you gave me the most incredible orgasm last night! You have great hands." Emerald purred as she scooted around so her back faced Romy. "How are things going with Thomas and his crew?"

After delicately removing Emerald's bikini top, Romy slathered her hands with coconut-scented sunscreen. She ran her hands over Emerald's smooth shoulders, cascading down her slim back. *Her body is like a work of art; the definition of her muscles is exquisite. And she has the softest skin I've ever felt.* Romy felt herself becoming distracted, and Emerald's question reminded her to return inside shortly to move ahead with her investigation.

Ignoring Emerald's mention of last night's tryst, which consisted of Romy finger fucking Emerald in her room, fully clothed. Since Romy had arrived weeks ago now, she and Emerald had sex within various parts of the mansion. But it was always the same; Romy fucking Emerald while never removing her clothing or receiving pleasure.

But strangely enough, this arrangement suited Romy well. She was naturally dominant in bed, and Romy typically identified herself as a top. And since these intimate encounters seemed to be considered part of her role as Emerald's body-guard, Romy assumed tunnel vision without expectations of reciprocation. She enjoyed giving the actress pleasure and seeing such joy on her face. But in order for Romy to let go and allow herself to be physically vulnerable, she needed a true connection. And that wasn't something Romy would get from a world-famous, closeted actress who was 20 years her senior. Their sexual relationship was purely transactional, but at least the boundaries were clear.

"That's what I wanted to talk to you about. This afternoon, I was going to attempt to procure video surveillance of the men who shot at us on Rodeo. Is there anything you wanted to do today, in particular? Because if not, I was going to work inside for a bit." Romy replied, wiping sunscreen on her thighs.

"Are there cameras on Rodeo Drive? Wow, I didn't know that, but I guess I should have since it seems like they're everywhere." Emerald turned to face Romy, looking surprised. "It would be great if something was captured."

"Oh yeah, on Rodeo alone, there are over 29 cameras in the area. And since we were on the corner of a major intersection, I do not doubt that we will find something." Romy grabbed the towel from her lounger, wiping the sweat from her brow.

Then, leaning closer to Emerald, she added, "But I still need to get clearance from the police and my security agency. So, I should get to work." As she stood to leave, Romy caught herself winking at Emerald, which surprised her. It was as though she was subconsciously flirting with Emerald while trying to maintain a professional front. *Man, I think she might be getting to me!*

Emerald waved her hand. "No, I'm happy staying at the estate. We are putting my parts in the movie on hold until this mess blows over, and for now, I have no desire to socialize. I feel safest here, with people that I trust and adore." Romy sensed that Emerald's tone was for her benefit. But even if the pair weren't traveling around Beverly Hills, Romy was still committed to doing her job.

Before Romy headed towards the backdoor, Emerald called out, "Romy? Tonight, after dinner, I'd like to see you in my room. It's a surprise, okay?"

Shaking her head, Romy chuckled and replied slightly sarcastically, "As you wish, princess. I can't imagine what it could be." But Romy knew what surprises Emerald had planned. *Hmmm, maybe I'll bring my toys for variety.*

Romy went inside, enjoying the cool air-conditioned interior, which contrasted sharply with the afternoon heat. Marilyn had gone shopping, leaving her and Emerald alone in the mansion. *No wonder Emerald feels lonely here. This place is massive, especially when it's empty.*

Romy thought about the stories Emerald told about her life when they would lie together at night. It was now customary for Romy to sleep beside Emerald in her bedroom, and the women had developed a routine. After Romy got Emerald off, she would snuggle into her, calm and at peace.

These were the moments that Romy loved the most. She enjoyed seeing Emerald's fragility and her gentleness. And Romy felt proud that she could inspire softness in Emerald, loosening her performative nature. One night, after a climatic session, Emerald shared about the first and only time that she had a girlfriend, which intrigued Romy. She never pegged Emerald as a committed person, especially not with her secret affairs. But the story had shed more light on Emerald, giving Romy a different perspective.

"We were starring in a movie and had been on set together for two months. We saw each other daily and spent much time chatting in my trailer between sets. She became my best friend in a short period of time, and we were always together."

Emerald spoke quietly, nestled in Romy's arms. "One night, after a particularly grueling scene that required a lot of physical strength, Lana, my friend, offered to massage my shoulders. I remember how much I loved her touch. After a few minutes, I reciprocated, wanting to explore her body further, but I would have never had the courage. But Lana, perhaps sensing my desire, slowly guided my hands down to her breasts, allowing my fingers to pinch her nipples gently."

Romy listened intently as she played with Emerald's hair. Emerald continued, "She said to me, 'kiss my neck as you play with my breasts.' So, I did, and to this day, I still remember her skin's sweet scent; she smelled like vanilla." Emerald turned to look up at Romy, adding, "We had sex, and I fell in love with Lana immediately. Shortly afterward, we started a secret relationship. Even though no one knew about us, my heart would burst with joy whenever we were together. That was the happiest time of my life."

"Wow, that sounds intense but beautiful," Romy commented. "Whatever happened to her? Obviously, you aren't together now, so how did it end?" Romy was curious as Emerald's voice was thick with emotion. She could tell that this was no ordinary affair.

She recognised the name Lana- surely Lana O'Brien, the movie star, but she kept that to herself. Emerald was trusting her with this, with something so personal and real for the first time.

Emerald sighed, shaking her head. "We wanted to make it work so badly, but neither of us had the courage to come out publicly. Lana was an up-and-coming Hollywood star and had also been invited to pose for Playboy. Between my established success and her job opportunities, we knew that announcing our relationship would mean career suicide."

Romy could see tears well in Emerald's eyes. "Eventually, she met a film director and got married. And shortly after that, I met my first husband. After that, it felt like this was the path I needed to take, although it ripped my heart out to know that Lana and I could never truly be together."

As Romy thought back to their late-night conversations, she felt conflicted. Part of her wanted to scoop Emerald in her arms and protect her from the world. But Emerald was also impulsive and fickle, even manipulative, albeit playfully. As the women grew closer, Romy oscillated between caring for Emerald and being slightly distrustful. Romy felt Emerald drawing her in, but she was concerned that this could affect her judgment and focus. *After all, I'm her bodyguard, not her best friend or her girlfriend. And I don't think I could be both.*

Starting at her laptop, Romy continued to research Thomas, paying special attention to his patterns. In her investigation, Romy learned that Thomas Black had a history of violence long before he met Emerald Crowle. In his late twenties, Thomas had been charged with domestic abuse but was never convicted. This is likely what caused the end of his time with the Marines.

In a separate case, five years later, the fitness trainer was involved in a lawsuit whereby the plaintiff accused Mr. Black of intimidation and vandalism because of late payments towards his gym membership. The case was settled out of court, with Mr. Black required to pay a fine.

Gathering documents, Romy began to organize her case file to have Thomas Black arrested. But until that happened, Emerald needed to remain on guard and required protection to keep her safe.

The afternoon turned to early evening, and the sky, which had started blue and bright, was becoming dull and cloudy. Romy looked out the window, noticing a few random drops hitting the pane. *Oh wow, it hardly ever rains here. I guess it's a good thing that we are staying in tonight.* Romy hadn't heard anything from Emerald since she went inside and had forgotten her request until she entered the dining hall, wrapped in a long, lacy transparent robe. Romy could tell that she was naked underneath.

"Hey, stranger. You've been working all day. Why don't you take a break and come join me upstairs? I have a surprise, remember?" Emerald gave Romy a coy smile, and Romy chuckled. Romy assumed that the actress was horny and wanted to be serviced.

Looking Emerald up and down, her eyes penetrating through the sheer material, Romy's mouth watered. Romy could practically taste Emerald as her gaze traveled down below Emerald's navel to her pubic bone. "I could use a break, and you look like a tasty snack," Romy quipped. "But pleasuring you is more of a given than a surprise, right?"

Emerald giggled, shaking her head. "I love how you know me so well. No, seriously, it's not what you think." Emerald motioned Romy to stand. "Come, follow me into my room. I swear that you'll be surprised. Do you trust me?"

I don't know about that. Still, Romy was intrigued; Emerald had a way of making the most mundane moments interesting, and curiosity got the best of Romy. Allowing Emerald to guide her, she was led into Emerald's master bedroom suite.

"Close the door behind you," Emerald ordered. "Marilyn is home, and I don't want her to disturb us." Romy faced Emerald as she presented a black silk tie. Emerald stated, "This is a blindfold. If you consent, I'd like you to wear it. Tonight, I'd like to pleasure *you*, to explore every inch of your body. I want to make you feel amazing, Romy. Will you let me?"

Romy's eyes widened. Until this moment, their intimacy had always been one-sided. And since Romy always assumed professionalism, it was easier for her to be the giver. Allowing herself to receive and to be vulnerable to Emerald's touch was a more intense experience for Romy. But Emerald appeared so genuine and enthusiastic, and her generosity was enticing.

Taking a deep breath, Romy agreed. "Okay, I'll

let you. But as you know, this is a little out of my comfort zone. I'm used to being in charge."

"That's why it's a surprise. It would be an honor to worship your body, to kiss you everywhere." Emerald's voice turned into a seductive whisper. "Close your eyes." Romy did as instructed and as the room went black, she felt the silk material wrap around her eyes. She heard the floor creak slightly as Emerald seemed to move behind her. Then, Romy felt a warm tickle against her earlobe. "Lift your arms; I want to undress you slowly."

Romy, who was wearing a cotton t-shirt, raised her arms, feeling Emerald's hands slide up her waist, grabbing the material. In one swift movement, Emerald removed Romy's shirt, leaving her in a sports bra and sweatpants. Delicate kisses danced across Romy's shoulders as Emerald dragged her fingertips down Romy's spine. Immediately, she shivered with delight. In her absence of sight, every sensation was heightened.

"I'm taking this off," Emerald stated, her voice tingling against Romy's skin. The sports bra had clasps in the back, and the actress easily unhooked Romy's undergarment. As Emerald freed her breasts, Romy felt bare and vulnerable, the most submissive she had ever been. She was grateful for the blindfold because otherwise, she would never have let go of control. Being showered with physical sensations without sight made it easier for Romy to remain in her body. As Emerald continued to kiss the nape of Romy's neck, with her tongue dragging down Romy's backbone, Emerald's hands traveled around Romy's torso, scaling upwards to caress Romy's breasts. Her nipples instantly responded to Emerald's touch as she gently pinched them. Then, running her tongue up Romy's neck, Emerald whispered, "I can't wait to strip you naked, to taste you. I want you to come in my mouth."

Romy swallowed, feeling herself grow wet with desire as she had so many times before for Emerald- but this time felt so different. She sighed, succumbing to Emerald's tempting hands. Deftly, Emerald removed Romy's sweatpants and then tugged at the waistband of her boxers, pulling both down to Romy's feet. Romy leaned back, allowing Emerald to hold her while she stepped out of her clothes. Romy was now completely naked and blindfolded, entirely at the mercy of Emerald's seduction.

"How do you feel?" Emerald softly asked. "Do

you like me taking the lead?" Romy licked her lips and nodded, enthralled with arousal. "Yeah, I do. You feel amazing." Her nipples hardened further, and goosebumps covered the surface of her skin. She felt Emerald move to the front as her lips sought Romy's. The women had never kissed on the mouth before; the sex between them had always been detached and transactional. But when Romy felt Emerald's lips touch hers, she felt a warm burst of energy as their mouths collided.

Emerald's tongue hungrily sought Romy's, and Romy could not hold back her passion. They kissed deeply as Emerald gently pulled back Romy's neck, planting her mouth on Romy's neck. Romy wanted to rip off the blindfold and grab Emerald to throw her on the bed. But Emerald could sense Romy's desire to top, saying, "No, you stay put. Stay just as you are. Tonight, I am making love to you; I only want you to receive my touch."

Romy's heart beat faster as Emerald moved her lips and hands down past Romy's breasts, pausing to suckle. As her mouth teased Romy's nipples, her hands traveled down past Romy's navel, resting on her pubic bone. "Open your legs for me. I want to feel you." Spreading her legs wider, Emerald's fingers inched below, exploring the folds of Romy's labia. "Oh my god, you are so wet!" Indeed, Romy could feel her pussy swell with juices, desiring more of Emerald. Then, as if she could read her mind, Emerald hooked her fingers, plunging inside Romy while raising her face to kiss her on the lips.

Romy's knees buckled with ecstasy as Emerald's fingers explored deep inside of her. She fell against Emerald as Emerald grabbed Romy's right leg, hooking it around her. "See? It's easier to fuck you like this when you have your leg wrapped around me."

Moans and sighs erupted from Romy as Emerald began to fuck her. Then, almost instantly, a wave of pleasure shot through Romy like a crescendo. "Oh god, oh my god!" Romy felt the release that had been building deep inside of her for a long time now. The orgasm burst deep inside Romy, causing her to bellow as her body shook. But Emerald kept her grip tight and laughed. "Mmm, good! I love to see you come. But I know you have more in you, and as I said, I want you to come in my mouth."

Romy felt lightheaded, so she lowered her leg to maintain her balance. She couldn't take not seeing Emerald anymore. "Take this off; I want to see you, please!" Emerald's fingers hooked around the silk material, sliding it off Romy's head. But before Romy could say anything, Emerald removed her fingers and brought them to Romy's lips. "Taste yourself while I kiss you." Romy opened her mouth, allowing Emerald's finger inside. Sucking, she could taste the earthy saltiness of her juices while Emerald's lips pressed against hers.

"Stay where you are; I'm getting on my knees for you." Emerald quickly grabbed a pillow off the bed as Romy looked down at her. She looked so beautiful in the dim light. This was her favorite Emerald, no make up, tousled hair, never more sexy, never more beautiful. Her lovely hazel eyes looked up longingly at Romy. Romy ran her hand through Emerald's golden hair, caressing her face. Emerald gave Romy a devilish look before grabbing Romy's hips. "I can't wait to taste you."

Romy closed her eyes, feeling Emerald's tongue gently teasing the head of her clit. Romy felt herself moaning loudly as Emerald moved to licking and sucking her pussy and when she felt Emerald's tongue push inside her she thought she would come instantly.

A warm, tingling sensation traveled up her

legs, and she felt herself begin to shake. Grabbing Emerald's head to steady herself, she ground herself against Emerald's mouth, greedy for more sensations. Her hips thrust as Emerald's tongue quickened its pace. "Oh yeah, right there, oh my god, yes! Please don't stop, fuck yes!"

Another orgasm began to brew inside, catapulting Romy into the throws of passion. As Emerald sucked on her clit, Romy could no longer control her ecstasy.

Throwing her head back, she roared with pleasure, pressing her pussy hard against Emerald's face. Romy felt as though a million fireworks were bursting inside her body. It was a climax like no other.

Panting, Romy tried to catch her breath as a mischievous-looking Emerald looked up at her. Then, appearing just as satisfied as Romy, Emerald licked her lips and said in a sly voice, "Oh, it was so hot to see you come in my mouth. And thank you —I always get what I want." Emerald winked, and Romy, still high from orgasm, looked down and laughed. "Yeah, apparently you do!"

Romy sat heavily on the ground, facing Emerald. "Fuck, I've never come that hard before in my life." Emerald grinned and leaned in. Romy met her halfway and their mouths became lost to each other in the moment.

Romy wasn't sure what was happening or what she was giving in to, but she knew she couldn't have stopped it if she had tried.

11

Emerald fluttered her eyes open, sensing movement beside her. After their intimate evening, Romy curled beside her and stroked Emerald's hair until they fell asleep. Then, as the sun shone through Emerald's sheer curtains, she heard Romy whisper in her ear, "Good morning. Did you sleep well?"

Emerald moved onto her back, stretching her arms. "Mmmm, I did. I'm sleeping so much better these days, having you in my bed to keep me company." Emerald rolled over to smile at Romy as she rose from her bed. "What time is it? Where are you going?"

Romy grinned down at Emerald. "It's still early;

it's almost 6:30 am, and I need to head to the gym." Emerald observed Romy as she hooked her sports bra behind her back, throwing on her t-shirt. Emerald couldn't help but notice the fine muscles of her body in the morning light.

Fuck, she looks so beautiful in the morning.

"Then I need to meet with the police chief. I think we are getting close to throwing Thomas in jail. We are comparing and cross-referencing evidence from his various files."

"Oh wow, that's good news." Emerald curled her body around her duvet. Emerald added, watching Romy dress, "I wish you could stay in bed with me. We could sleep in and have breakfast together. Did you have fun with me last night?"

Romy met Emerald's gaze, her expression hard to read. "I did. Thanks for a great night. But I need to leave for a bit. Work comes before play, and I miss working out. I haven't been to the gym in three days."

Emerald was slightly disappointed, although she didn't want to make it obvious. "Okay, well, enjoy your morning. I have a call with my agent at 10:00 am. Apparently, we need to meet with the director in a few days to discuss where we are at with the movie."

"I'll let you sleep more. But text me when you are up and let me know if you need to leave the mansion. I'll return before that so that I can accompany you," Romy reassured Emerald, but the actress shook her head. "No, I'm good here. But you'll need to come with me to the meeting."

Romy leaned in and kissed Emerald on the forehand before leaving her bedroom. "Of course. I'll see you soon."

As soon as Romy left, pangs of loneliness hit Emerald in the chest. She thought about the fact that Thomas may quickly go to jail and what that might mean for her and Emerald. While the actress was excited at the possibility that her life would soon return to normal, Emerald was also aware that without Thomas in the picture, there was no reason for Romy to stay. *Shit! I guess that means she'll be leaving soon. God, I wish there was a way I could entice her to stay.*

Hugging her pillow, Emerald thought about the night before and how she loved worshiping every inch of Romy's lean, toned body. The taste of Romy still lingered on Emerald's tongue as she craved more of her. As Emerald lay in bed, she thought about her life and intermittent lovers. Between husbands, Emerald always found solace in the arms of the beautiful women she encountered. But no one had her heart since Lana, that is, until she met Romy.

Emerald knew she was falling for her bodyguard and she was struggling with what that might mean. Lines had been crossed by both of them. Many lines, both professional and personal. Well and truly crossed.

She tossed and turned for the next few hours, wishing to fall back asleep, but her stomach was in knots, knowing that, soon, Romy could be gone. The thought was too much for Emerald to bear.

Maybe it is time for something different, Emerald thought to herself.

I'll ask Romy if she wants to be my girlfriend. Like real girlfriend. Then when she doesn't need to be my bodyguard anymore, she can be my girlfriend instead.

Once she was resolute in her decision, Emerald could finally rest until her agent Chet called at 10:00 am. During their phone meeting, Chet set the time for the meeting with the film director, which was to be the following day. They would gather at Crystalline, a swanky lounge in the heart of the Hollywood studios. The venue was known for its expansive rooftop bar, which was a popular meeting spot for directors, actors, and screenplay writers.

"I'll be bringing Romy with me," Emerald stated to Chet, who responded, "No problem, babe. How is that working out for you?" Emerald was aware that Chet was referring to her issues with Thomas; after all, it was Chet who arranged Emerald's bodyguard.

Emerald thought to herself, *Well, I'm getting laid regularly, so it's working out well in that way!* But out loud, she replied, "It's been great. Romy is very professional, and I certainly feel safer with her around. And it shouldn't be too long before the police arrest Thomas, or so, that's what Romy told me."

"Good, good. I'm glad to hear it. See you tomorrow at 11:00 am. Oh, and make sure you look your best." Chet and Emerald said their goodbyes and ended the call. Emerald felt renewed; she needed to be back on set after all of the drama with Thomas. And she was looking forward to bringing Romy tomorrow, even more excited to have her as a partner potentially.

Emerald finally left her bedroom in search of Marilyn. She requested that a special meal be prepared, by candlelight, outside in the garden. "I want the most romantic setting that you can imagine." Marilyn agreed without question and Emerald considered how lucky she was that although her housekeeper was aware of her affair with Romy, as a loyal employee, Marilyn would never speak out of line or ask about her personal life.

After spending the early part of the afternoon suntanning by the pool and rehearsing what she would say to Romy, Emerald decided to treat herself with a trip to Verve salon. She knew it was risky to travel alone without Romy, but Emerald felt restless, and she wanted time to be alone with her thoughts before dinner. The actress always felt most confident when she was fully coiffed, and as she explained to Heather, her hairstylist, tonight would be a special occasion.

"Oh my, well, that's exciting! So who's the lucky fellow?" Heather added a spritz of hairspray to Emerald's blowout, keeping the hairs in place.

Emerald thought quickly. While she and Heather were close in a customer service manner, Heather was excluded from the details of Emerald's personal life. She wished she could be more candid as her heart burst with love for Romy. But Emerald couldn't risk the negative attention, should the secret of her sexuality be leaked to the public.

"Oh, um, I'm meeting with my film director tonight. There's been a lot of chaos with the recent filming, so we are gathering to discuss how to move forward." Emerald glossed over the question before adding, "It's an important talk, and I want to look my best."

Heather nodded. "Wow, it sounds like a big deal. Best of luck, my dear." Emerald peered at her reflection, shaking her hair. "I love it, Heather. Thanks so much." Emerald left the salon feeling fresh and inspired as she returned home to prepare for her date.

Hours later, while finishing her makeup, Emerald heard a knock at her bedroom door. "Hey Emerald, it's Romy. Can I come in?"

"Of course!" Emerald's heart fluttered to greet Romy. "Perfect timing. Dinner will be served in the garden soon." Romy lingered in the doorway as Emerald thought to herself, *God, she is so handsome! I wish I could just rip off her t-shirt right now!* But to Emerald's surprise, Romy looked concerned. "You look different. Did you go anywhere today?"

Giving Romy a coy smile, Emerald replied,

"Yes, I went to see Heather at Verve." Then, turning her head, she added, "Do you like it?"

Romy sighed, shaking her head. She approached Emerald and crouched in front of her. "You shouldn't have done that. It's dangerous for you to be out alone. I wish you had called me. I would've come with you."

Grabbing Romy's hands, Emerald apologized, "I know. I'm sorry. It was a last-minute decision. But nothing happened. I was fine." Romy's expression softened. "It's okay, but your safety is my utmost concern; it's why you hired me. So please don't do that again, at least not before Thomas is arrested."

"I understand. I promise I won't." Then, changing the subject, Emerald stated, "Why don't you get ready for dinner, and I'll meet you in the garden."

Romy nodded. "Sure, I'm excited about this dinner. I'm absolutely starving. I'll grab a quick shower and meet you out there."

Moments later, the women were seated outside as Marilyn placed two filet mignon dinners in front of their place settings. Emerald was impressed with the table. There was a large bouquet of fresh flowers as a centerpiece, and the candles provided a warm glow. "Marilyn, this looks incredible. Thank you so much."

"Yes, thanks. This looks like an incredible meal," Romy echoed Emerald's sentiments. Marilyn smiled, bowing her head. "Enjoy, ladies. I'll be inside; call me if you need anything."

Once Marilyn left, Emerald looked at Romy. "Um, before we begin, I'd like to talk to you. I have something important that I want to share." Emerald was typically confident, and there wasn't much that could rattle her. But as she stared into Romy's lovely blue eyes, Emerald felt nervous.

Romy put down her glass and leaned in closer. "Sure. What's on your mind? Is it about Thomas?"

Shaking her head, Emerald replied, "No, no. It's nothing like that." Taking a deep breath and gathering her courage, Emerald continued, "Romy, I-I'm falling in love with you. I know that this wasn't supposed to be a romantic arrangement. But after all the time we've spent, and the times we've been intimate, I can't deny my desire. I haven't felt this way since my first and only girl-friend, Lana."

Emerald paused to observe Romy's expression. Romy froze in her seat, looking stunned.

I can't read her. Does she understand what I'm trying to say?

Emerald continued, reaching across to grab Romy's hand, feeling that the conversation needed more clarification. "I know that Thomas will be arrested soon, and then, I won't have any reason for a bodyguard. But I don't want you to leave. I'd love it if we could continue seeing each other outside of this role. Would you like to be my girlfriend? Of course, it would have to be a secret relationship. But I've done that before. I can do it again."

Emerald exhaled. It was a relief to share her feelings with Romy finally. But Romy still appeared aghast, stoic in her seat. Giggling nervously, Emerald prodded, "What do you think? Please say something."

With eyes wide, Romy exclaimed, "Are you kidding? You want to have a relationship? Emerald, I thought this was all business. You lead me to believe that fucking you was part of my job." Shaking her head, Romy's expression turned from confused to hurt. "I'm not like you. I'm an out and proud lesbian. I've never been in the closet, and I never will. Secret sex with you as part of my job is one thing, but I can't be your dirty little secret forever. I care deeply for you, but I just can't be your *secret* girlfriend."

Furrowing her brow with disgust, Romy added, "So, basically, you just want to use me behind closed doors but pretend you don't know me in public? No, that will never work for me."

Emerald's jaw dropped. "No, no, you don't understand. I *love* you! I need you, Romy. Don't you feel the same? The other night was magical. I *know* there is a connection."

Romy sighed, placing her napkin on the table. "Listen, I don't mind working for you. It's definitely been one of the more interesting jobs I've had. And yes, you are attractive and sexy. I've allowed myself to be seduced by your charms." Romy crossed her muscular arms and added, "But I'm not in love with you. And if I'm going to be in a relationship, I want to give my all to my partner and celebrate our love openly. You're not that way, Emerald. It's just not possible."

Emerald stared at Romy and her hard blue eyes, processing the conversation. She had never been rejected by a conquest before, and it felt as though she had just got slapped in the face. Emerald blinked, feeling tears begin to well in her eyes. *Don't fucking cry! Don't you dare cry in front of her.*

The table was silent for a few seconds before Emerald found her voice. Averting eye contact, she stated shakily, "Okay, fine. I didn't mean to offend you. We'll keep it strictly business." Clearing her throat, Emerald straightened her shoulders and picked up her cutlery. She could feel Romy's eyes on her, but Emerald didn't look up. Instead, she concentrated on cutting her steak.

Romy spoke in a mild tone. "It's okay. Like I said, I like being here. And I want to keep you safe. I'm really sorry, Emerald." An uncomfortable pause ballooned, and Emerald nodded silently. After finishing her steak, Emerald rose from the table, announcing, "I'm going to my room. I have an early meeting with the film director tomorrow. And you're coming with me. So get some rest. I'll see you in the morning."

Leaving Romy alone at the table, Emerald excused herself and walked inside. Her heart ached, and her face burned with humiliation. She traveled upstairs without a word to Marilyn. Emerald knew that she needed her sleep, but a peaceful slumber would not find her tonight.

Tears streamed from her eyes onto the pillow.

12

Romy stared at her half-eaten plate with a vanished appetite. With Emerald now gone, Romy sat alone in the garden, watching the flames from the candles smolder and diminish. She sat frozen in her seat, confused and angry. But another emotion was bubbling beneath the surface that Romy couldn't yet identify.

Unlike Emerald, Romy didn't want to rely on Marilyn to clear the table. Romy hadn't hired the housekeeper, so she felt it was only polite and respectful to help bring some dishes. Her legs felt wobbly as she stood; the conversation between her and Emerald made Romy feel weak and tired. Her heart felt gutted because she was looking forward to spending time with Emerald. But Romy was also insulted by Emerald's proposal, and unfortunately, she couldn't control her strong emotional reaction.

What did I think was going to happen? I've become unprofessional and I've gotten myself into this mess.

Stacking the plates and lying the silverware across, Romy carried the dishes inside, using the side entrance, which gave better access to the kitchen. There, she found Marilyn scrubbing away in front of a bubbly basin. "Oh, hi. I wanted to bring these inside for you," Romy greeted the housekeeper. "Where should I leave them?"

Marilyn looked up from the sink. "Hello, my dear. Oh, please don't worry. I can take care of those. I'll go outside to take down the table." But Romy insisted on helping. "I really don't mind. You prepared us a lovely meal, and it's my pleasure to tidy up."

Marilyn smiled gently. "I'm so glad you enjoyed it. Is Emerald still outside?" Romy gulped and shook her head, unsure of what to say. "Um, no. She, um, wasn't feeling well, so she decided to lay down after dinner."

"Oh no! I hope everything is alright." Then, wiping her hands on an apron, Marilyn added,

"She has been under so much stress since the divorce. And I know she's had a terrible time sleeping. So I think it's great that you are here for her. I think having you at the house calmed her considerably."

Romy fought the urge to laugh; Emerald seemed the exact opposite of calm to her. But it was one of the qualities that charmed Romy. As much as it confused her, Romy appreciated how expressive Emerald was with her desires. Being so forthcoming and vulnerable was something Romy struggled with in all of her relationships. "Well, I'm glad to hear that because I take my job seriously, and my clients are my number one focus."

"But it's more than that. I also think that having someone keep her company has been good for her healing. Emerald may be one of the most recognizable actresses in North America. And fans don't equal friends." Marilyn bustled around the kitchen. "People like Emerald don't have a close social circle because they need to be on guard. She is a very lonely person. And I think your presence has helped her remove some of her walls."

"She is a fascinating woman, that's for sure," Romy mused, although she didn't want Marilyn to pick up on her bitterness. "But we are getting close to having Thomas arrested. My investigation is complete, and I am finalizing my file on him. So, soon, he won't be a problem anymore."

Marilyn breathed a sigh of relief. "Oh, that's wonderful to hear. And I guess that means you'll be leaving us soon. Do you think you and Emerald will stay in touch? If it were up to me, you would be welcome here anytime."

Romy beamed at the housekeeper. Marilyn was so warm and kind. But Romy knew that her time with Emerald was coming to an end. "That's so sweet, thank you. But, to be honest, I'm not sure. It depends on where my next assignment will be and if I need to travel out of the state." That wasn't a lie, per se. Her schedule was intense, and she was rarely in the same place for long, depending on the client's requirements. But Marilyn only needed to hear part of the story, and Romy wouldn't out Emerald to anyone.

Marilyn approached Romy, putting a hand on her arm. "It would be nice for Emerald if you *did* stay in touch. You two seem to get along so well." There was a curious sparkle in Marilyn's eyes as she stared at Romy. Her voice seemed suggestive as if Marilyn knew more than she was letting on.

But Romy kept her tone neutral and diplomatic. "You never know what the future holds. But for now, I want to focus on Thomas' arrest." Glancing at the clock on the wall, she realized it was becoming late. "Oh, I need to accompany Emerald to her meeting tomorrow morning. I should go to bed too. Thanks again for dinner."

The housekeeper bid Romy good night as she traveled up the stairs to her own bedroom. Tonight, she wouldn't be sharing a bed with Emerald, which gutted Romy. As she removed her clothes to prepare for bed, Romy thought back to last night with Emerald. She had shown Romy such a generous and sensual side of herself as she worshiped Romy's body. Their lovemaking had been so different from the last times Romy and Emerald had been intimate. Emerald's touch felt gentle and soft; her energy filled with care.

Unlike past experiences where sex seemed transactional, Emerald focused solely on her pleasure, allowing Romy to melt into the moment. Thinking back, it now seemed like a dream, and Romy realized how much she had been holding back emotionally with Emerald.

I'm truly sad at the idea of losing her; we have an undeniable connection. But our lives could never sync with Emerald in the closet. And I could never share her in secret while she has other men in her life. Fuck!

Romy's heart was caught between how she felt about the actress and the reality of Emerald's situation. She stared at the ceiling, mulling over her choices. Romy could leave Emerald for good after completing the assignment with Thomas or try to move forward with a relationship. But neither option seemed right, and the more Romy played with the various scenarios in her head, the more frustrated she became. *It's just not possible; I can't do this. I just can't!* Romy began to cry in bed, hugging her pillow and soaking it with tears. The exhaustion of her heartbreak was enough to eventually lull her to a fitful sleep.

Beep, beep, beep! The following day, Romy woke up with a start to the sound of her alarm. She felt exhausted and emotionally drained as remnants of abstract dreams fluttered through her consciousness, dissipating with the morning sun. Romy quickly sat up in bed, rubbing her puffy eyes. "Oh god, I need to get ready for this appointment," she groaned to herself, "Fuck, this is going to be so awkward." Then, with her stomach in knots, Romy leaped out of bed, selecting an outfit for today.

She knew it was an important day for Emerald,

and Romy wanted to present herself profession-
ally. She pulled a black suit off the rack, sweeping
it with a lint brush. *Yup, that's perfect. The suit will
add style, but it still makes me look like a bodyguard.
There should be clarity about who I am and why I'm
accompanying Emerald to this meeting.*

Behind her closed bedroom door, Romy could
hear the sound of a hairdryer from next door,
signaling that Emerald was awake. Romy's heart
lurched as she resisted the urge to visit Emerald in
her room. Sighing aloud, she spoke to herself, "No,
it's best that I leave her alone. I need to focus on
my assignment, and Emerald needs to focus on
this meeting." Romy's body felt heavy as she
cascaded down the stairs, greeted by the smell of
freshly brewed coffee.

"Good morning, dear. How did you sleep?"
Marilyn asked, chipper as ever. Romy didn't dare
express her misery, instead choosing to lie. "It was
great, thanks. And this coffee smells divine."

Marilyn grinned. "Enjoy. Emerald should be
downstairs soon, and Jesse will come in 45 minutes
to pick her up. I'm guessing you'll be driving
behind, right?" Romy nodded, picking up her mug.
She sipped on her brew, keeping her gaze low.

Anxiously, she waited for Emerald to join her in the dining room.

Over the past weeks, they had developed a routine of enjoying their morning coffee together; for Romy, it was a pleasant way to start the day. But this morning, Romy wasn't sure that would happen. Her heart ached at the thought of losing the small comforts that had developed between her and Emerald.

"Marilyn? Jesse should be here soon. Could you fix me a fruit plate, please?" Romy was startled by the sound of Emerald's voice as she cascaded down the staircase. Romy glanced at the actress, eyeing the silky white slip dress that hugged Emerald's perfect curves. The dress was short enough to show off the actress's shapely legs but still classy enough for a daytime look. Emerald's beautiful blond hair was voluminous, curly, and rich. As Emerald reached the bottom stair, she threw on a matching blazer, her six-inch stilettos *click-clacking* on the marble floors. Romy gulped, her face blushing at the sight of Emerald's beauty. Not for the first time, Romy was speechless.

Emerald briefly made eye contact with Romy, stating in an icy tone, "We're leaving soon. I need you to drive behind myself and Jesse. Got it?"

Romy bobbed her head, straightening her tie. "Yes, I understand. I'm ready to go whenever Jesse arrives."

Marilyn set a plate of fresh, tropical fruits in front of Emerald and turned to Romy. "Did you want anything before you leave?" Romy shook her head; the anxiety brewing in her stomach had killed her appetite. "No thanks, I appreciate it." Avoiding eye contact, Emerald sat in front of Romy, spearing a slice of cantaloupe with a fork. Finally, after a few moments, Emerald spoke, "How did you sleep? I'm guessing it was nice to be back in your own bed, huh?"

Romy couldn't tell if Emerald was being sarcastic; the truth was that Romy slept horribly. But she knew better than to share her truth. So instead, she replied, "I slept well, thanks. You?"

Stretching her arms wide, Emerald replied, "So good. I forgot how much I loved taking up space in my bed. And it was nice not to have to deal with snoring."

Romy recognized the jab, ignoring Emerald's comment. Instead, she rose from the table. "I'm going to wait in the front foyer. I'll hop in my vehicle and follow you when Jesse arrives."

"Cool," Emerald replied curtly, focusing her

attention on the fruit plate. Then, sighing audibly, Romy strolled away from the table, feeling uncomfortable. *God, I can't wait to get out of here. The tension in this house is too much.*

Thirty minutes later, Jesse arrived to pick Emerald up, and with Romy trailing close behind, the group soon reached Crystalline. Romy watched as Emerald exited the back seat and strolled towards the lounge. Romy took it as her cue to get out of her car and follow Emerald, maintaining two feet of distance between them. As Romy noticed Emerald approaching the entrance, she turned to look behind her, holding the door open for Romy. "Thanks," Romy said, with the actress nodding her acknowledgement.

The group reached the rooftop patio, which was empty except for a bald, overly tanned gentleman in a checked suit and a short, younger-looking man in a plain black t-shirt. The checkered suit beamed at Emerald as she glided across the patio. "Emerald, my dear! You look stunning." Romy watched Emerald and the bald man kiss on the cheeks before Emerald introduced her security.

"Chet, darling. It's *so* lovely to see you!" Then, pointing to Romy, Emerald noted, "This is my

bodyguard. She'll be hanging out in the background while we talk business."

Emerald's agent appeared just as Romy imagined him—bald, loud, and bronze with a set of
pearly-white dentures. To Romy, he looked like a
used car salesman, although she was also aware
that Chet Walker was one of Hollywood's top
movie star agents. "Nice to meet ya, Romy." He
pumped the guard's hand, exclaiming, "My, that's
some handshake on you!" Chet turned to the
younger gentleman, saying, "Rory, Emerald, no
introductions are necessary for you two, correct?"

Emerald leaned in for him to kiss her cheek,
gleaming at him with a charming smile. "Of *course
not!* Thanks so much for meeting with us. I'm
excited to get back on track with this project." Chet
motioned for the group to sit down, but Romy
preferred to stand to keep an eye on her surroundings. She slipped on her aviator sunglasses and
held her arms crossed in front.

Emerald and her entourage chatted and
laughed for what seemed like hours; Romy was
bored, wishing she was at the gym.

Once the meeting had ended, Emerald stood
up and announced, "Chet, we'd like some privacy,
please," as she pointed to Romy and herself.

Emerald rarely needed to say more when explaining a request. Romy knew what would be coming next, and even with the tension between them, Romy had to admit that Emerald's power and authority greatly aroused her.

"Of course, my dear. I'll follow up on the details of what we discussed." Chet gathered Rory as the men left the patio. "Pleasure to meet you, Romy. Enjoy the day, ladies!"

Once the two women were alone, Emerald turned to seduce Romy. She patted the seat beside her and offered, "Come sit beside me. I know last night was tough on both of us. I understand you don't want to be in a secret relationship." Then, biting her bottom lip and batting her lashes, she added, "But you did mention that you didn't mind the job as it is, right?"

Romy froze, unsure of what to do. The confusion caused her mind to race in different directions. She felt her emotions spiral while her libido revved; having sex with Emerald was an exquisite experience, and her essence was intoxicating.

Brushing her dark hair out of her face, Romy nodded. "Um, yeah, that's true. I *did* say that. So, what do you want from me, Emerald? You want me to fuck you right here, on this rooftop patio?"

Romy was being partly sarcastic, but she was pretty confident that Emerald was serious.

"Hmmm, mmm!" Emerald's eyes penetrated Romy, boring into her soul. As the women locked eyes, Emerald slowly began to lift her slip dress, teasing Romy with a subtle flash of her shaved pussy. "I'm not wearing any underwear either, so it's easy to access for your magical hands." The actress slinked lower into the couch, out of view as Romy approached closer.

Fuck, she is driving me crazy.

Even though Romy was looming over Emerald, she felt as though Emerald was hunting her, luring Romy closer with suggestive movements.

Once Romy sat beside Emerald, Emerald slid a single strap off her right shoulder, slipping the material down past her breast and exposing a nipple. "Come here," Emerald whispered, "Suck on it; I want you to *feel me*, Romy. I want your hands all over my body. That's an order."

Filled with chaotic desire, Romy couldn't hold back any longer. She knew this was Emerald's way of maintaining control after rejection, but she couldn't help her own arousal that was overtaking her. Emerald's magnetic energy hypnotized Romy, and her sexual prowess was an undeniable force.

Wordlessly, Romy kneeled on the couch and put a palm between Emerald's breasts, lowering her further into the patio furniture. Then, with her other hand, she lifted Emerald's dress so that the bottom half of her body was available. Emerald giggled at Romy's dominant move, succumbing to her power.

"If you want me to fuck you, you need to lay right there and be quiet. Don't say a word; just take it. Okay?" Romy ordered, feeling assertive and disconnected. If she were going to be used like a sex toy, then Romy would behave like one, void of emotion or softness.

Emerald closed her eyes, sighing, "Yeah, okay. Take me however you want me, fuck me until I come hard for you." Romy looked down and grabbed Emerald's thigh, moving them apart. Usually, she would have wanted to taste Emerald first, to lick the glistening dew that formed along the lips of her vulva. But today, Romy didn't want to engage in foreplay. Instead, she spat on Emerald's pussy, taking two fingers to smear her saliva around Emerald's luscious lips.

Emerald moaned and writhed her body, beckoning Romy inside. Romy slid three fingers into her mouth to wet them before carefully sliding them inside Emerald, who was already so wet with desire.

Emerald moaned so loudly in pleasure and the sound of her drove Romy crazy.

Romy felt Emerald opening up for her, desperate for her. Keeping one palm on her chest to hold her in place, Romy pushed her hand deeper, responding to the motion of Emerald's thrusting hips. She added a fourth finger and began to fuck Emerald hard, just like she knew Emerald loved it. Looking down at Emerald, her soul felt hollow. This wasn't the kind of sex she enjoyed, transactional and cold. But due to her own fault, fucking Emerald had become part of her job, so Romy put on her best performance. But inside, Romy broke apart as she realized she loved Emerald. There was no realistic way to be together; Romy was settling, which crushed her heart.

As she robotically thrust her hand inside Emerald, Emerald's skin flushed, and her body started to twitch. Emerald liked it hard, very hard, and Romy was more than capable of giving her what she wanted. Romy watched her body respond and knew that she was close to orgasm. She licked the fingers of her own left hand and then lowered her left hand to join her right. She took the index finger of her left hand and circled it around Emerald's asshole, teasing the sensitive area. She pushed her finger deep inside Emerald's ass while maintaining the fucking of her pussy with her right hand. The penetration of her anus caused Emerald to buck wildly, groaning with pleasure. "Yes, yes, oh yes, I'm coming, fuck, don't stop, please!"

Romy felt the hot gush of Emerald's pleasure flood the palm of her right hand.

Romy fingered her roughly until her body was racked with muscular contractions and her head rolled back in ecstasy. Then, very slowly, Romy slid out of her once her climax had calmed. Still looking over her, Romy waited until Emerald's breath had returned to normal and her body relaxed.

Emerald opened her eyes and smiled, squealing, "Oh my god, that was so hot! Thank you!" But as Emerald sat up, Romy stood straight, wiped her hand on her pants and responded, "Cool. I'm heading back to the car. I'll wait for you and Jesse to leave the parking lot before I follow behind."

Romy turned on her heel to exit the patio, leaving Emerald disheveled on the couch. Once inside her vehicle, Romy felt ill, knowing she had

13

"Thank you, Jesse. We'll resume filming my scenes soon, so my agent will be in touch about your schedule for next week." Emerald exited the vehicle, feeling strange. Her sexual encounter with Romy was still on her mind, but it felt so different from the previous times they had been intimate. Even though Emerald's body responded as usual and was absolutely able to climax, Romy's touch felt distant and cold and as physically close as Romy was to Emerald, an invisible void had developed between them.

"How did it go?" Marilyn asked as Emerald entered the foyer. Marilyn had always supported

Emerald, and she knew Emerald was eager to return to work.

"It was fabulous; Rory is going to reschedule my set times and change my routine. We think that should keep Thomas away, especially if he doesn't know when I'll be shooting on location." Emerald heard a rustle behind her as Romy walked in. Turning slightly to address her, she added, "And Romy believes that the police should be able to arrest Thomas soon."

Gleefully, Marilyn clapped her hands together as Romy cleared her throat. "Yup, that's true. Soon, Thomas Black will no longer be a problem." Romy motioned to Emerald. "Could I speak to you alone for a moment?"

Emerald gulped and nodded as an ominous feeling came over her. She wasn't sure why, but she had a sense that whatever Romy was able to tell her wouldn't be happy news. "Sure. Would you like to sit in the garden where we had dinner?"

"Okay. I'll meet you out there in about ten minutes." Romy strolled upstairs while Emerald remained below. Marilyn then asked, "Could I fix you both something? Maybe some tea and fruit plates?"

Absentmindedly, Emerald bobbed her head,

void of an appetite. Ever since their chat at dinner, Emerald felt off. Her insomnia had returned in the absence of Romy in her bed. She felt humiliated and sad, knowing Romy didn't want to have a secret affair. But deep down, Emerald was aware that what she was asking of Romy was unfair. Emerald would've felt the same if she were in Romy's shoes. But it didn't take away from the fact that she was in love with Romy. But as she well knew, the price of love for someone like her, was pain. Sighing, she replied to Marilyn, "I'll be waiting outside."

Strolling into the garden, Emerald positioned herself on a piece of patio furniture. As she leaned back against the wicker material, Emerald thought about her life and the fleeting affairs that helped her to connect to her sexuality. Aside from clandestine trysts, Emerald had never given herself the opportunity to form healthy, intimate relationships with women. And besides Lana, her lovers were superficial, thrilled at the chance to have sex with a famous actress. In turn, Emerald also used them to give her what no man could ever provide.

Anxiety coursed through her blood as she waited for Romy to join her. Lost in thought,

Emerald jumped as soon as Romy's shadow cast over her. "Can I join you?"

"Yes, please, sit down. How did you enjoy the meeting this morning?" Emerald asked, easing into small talk. Since the dinner, the women barely spoke, and suddenly, Emerald felt shy.

Romy eased herself into the wicker chair. "To be honest, I wasn't listening. My attention was on the surrounding patio, so I could be aware of what was happening around us." Then, giving Emerald a playful smirk, she added, "You know that's my job, right?"

Emerald chuckled softly, her eyes meeting Romy's. "Yeah, I know. But you definitely paid attention to my body after the meeting." Emerald wanted to touch Romy's hand, to be close to her in mind and spirit, not just physically. But Romy's energy felt opposing, so she didn't dare.

Romy closed her eyes, remaining silent. Emerald wished that she could read Romy's mind. But instead, she allowed a few minutes to pass before asking, "What did you want to talk about?"

Romy opened her eyes and looked towards the sky. Then, inhaling deeply, she responded, "Emerald, I can't do this anymore. I'm sorry." Emerald furrowed her brow as her heart filled with panic.

"What do you mean? I know you can't be my girl-friend, but I still need a bodyguard."

Looking Emerald in the eye, Romy continued, "I've spoken to the police. The station has all the evidence, and we expect the arrest to happen within the next day or two. At that point, you won't need a bodyguard any longer." Emerald held eye contact with Romy as she processed the information.

"Oh, I see! Well, I mean, that's great news." Emerald tried to sound happy. Knowing that Thomas would no longer be threatening her was positive, but it came at the expense of losing Romy. She was conflicted with her emotions, and her heart felt like it was breaking in two. "So, I guess that's it, huh?"

Romy put her hand on Emerald's knee. "It *is* great news, Emerald. You are such a beautiful and prolific public figure; no one deserves to live in fear of violence, especially you. I'm so glad I got to meet and protect you." Pursing her lips together, shaking her head, Romy added, "But the time has come for me to leave. I can't offer you anything more. And I can't continue to be your sexual play-thing. I love you, Emerald, but our time has come to an end. I really wish things were different, and I know I'm going to miss you."

Tears sprouted in Emerald's eyes as she grabbed Romy's hand. "I wish I could come out. I love you too. But I can't, Romy. I just can't. My career and reputation is my life's work. I can't lose that. Even the more progressive filmmakers are dictated by these archaic rules and perceptions." Emerald's throat grew tight, knowing she was about to cry. "I'm going to miss you too. Even though I'll be safe from Thomas, I hate that this is happening right now." Finally, she could no longer hold back as a sob escaped. "Please don't go, Romy! Please, I need you."

Romy grabbed Emerald and pulled her in for a tight embrace. Emerald allowed herself to sink into the powerful arms of her bodyguard, her body convulsing with sorrow. Romy stroked Emerald's hair, trying to soothe her. They held each other in silence until Romy pulled away to look at Emerald.

"You are going to be just *fine*. You are strong, a fighter. Look at your success and everything you've achieved in the toughest industry." Romy tried to reassure Emerald. "There is a reason why we met each other, and I promise that I won't forget you. Without the fear of Thomas, you can move on with your life. And I'm sure you will soon meet someone who fits your lifestyle and limitations."

Romy stood up, pulling Emerald to stand with her. "Now, I need to show you something. Come with me." Emerald followed Romy into the house. Romy guided her into the dining room, where she noticed a plain, white plastic bag.

Romy dug in to retrieve a small, circular device, handing it to Emerald. The actress held it in her palm, noticing the black square base that featured a round, red button on top. To Emerald, the object looked like a buzzer one would see on a game show. Turning it around on her hand, she asked, "What is it?"

"It's a special alarm for you to always keep to yourself. If you find yourself in danger, press it, and it will signal an emergency request for the police," Romy explained. "The police force is aware of Thomas and his associates. If they receive notice from you via the alarm, the police will know it's an emergency, and they will arrive at whatever location you are at immediately."

Emerald nodded. "Wow, that's interesting. I didn't even know they made these kinds of gadgets. But you said the police are close to arresting Thomas, right?"

"Yes, but just in case something happens between now and then." Romy's eyes pierced through Emerald. "Even though I need to leave you, your safety is still my priority. I promised to protect you, and I want you to have this. So keep it on yourself at all times."

Emerald sighed, feeling gutted. Clutching the alarm, she reached for Romy, hugging her one last time. She inhaled the scent of her cologne, pressing her lips to Romy's neck, nuzzling against her skin. Emerald's voice shook with emotion. "I'm going to miss you so fucking much. My heart is seriously breaking."

Romy's face remained neutral, although Emerald noticed a deep sadness in her eyes. She knew that Romy cared for her and that there was a mutual attraction; she sensed their bond. "I know, Em. I feel the same way. But I've got to go." Romy squeezed Emerald one last time before moving away and turning on her heel. Emerald noticed a large black duffle bag parked by the front entrance. She couldn't believe that Romy was leaving for good.

She stood in the foyer wordlessly, watching as Romy grabbed the duffle, slinging it over her shoulder. The silence was deafening as Emerald

14

Romy struggled to keep her sorrow inside as she crossed the threshold of Emerald's front door into the long, winding driveway. But once she knew she was out of sight, Romy burst into tears, knowing she could never return. Her love for Emerald was real, but knowing they could never be a proper couple was more than Romy could bear. *No, this is for the best. I deserve an authentic relationship and a loving partner who is proud to be with me, and Emerald can't be that woman.*

The duffle bag seemed exceptionally heavy as Romy pulled on the straps. She traveled down the winding driveway towards her SUV, which was parked at the base of the estate. Romy intentionally parked further away from the house in an effort to throw off Thomas should he have wanted to pay a threatening visit.

Yesterday, when Romy was at the police station, she had spoken to Detective Spencer Wilde, who was leading the investigation. Upon finalizing the file on Thomas Black, Romy had met with the detective, who provided advice during the interim of Thomas being arrested.

"In knowing his patterns, you will want to deviate and give yourself space to avoid attracting danger. And because he knows your vehicle, he'll be looking for it, most likely to retaliate," Detective Wilde had stated. "At this point, we know he is hiding out in the Valley, Encino, to be exact. We've put a tracker on a car that we suspect is being shared between him and his gang of thugs."

"Okay, that's good to know. I'm supposed to follow Ms. Crowle and her driver to a lounge in Hollywood for a meeting." The detective retrieved an object from his desk. "Here, take this and give it to Ms. Crowle. It's a special emergency alarm she can use to contact us."

Furrowing her brow, Romy had asked, "Do you think it's safe for Ms. Crowle to be alone, just with the alarm? Or should I remain on assignment until Thomas is behind bars?"

Officer Wilde had shrugged, placing his meaty hands on his desk. "You're the expert, so I can't say. But I can tell you that we have enough evidence to arrest him. We just need to catch him, but hopefully, the tracker will lead our team to his whereabouts." Pointing at the gadget, the detective added, "And a buzzer is a great tool as well. You never know what can happen in these situations, but I think we have all our bases covered now."

Romy had felt relieved, knowing that the police unit was stepping in. But, as her love for Emerald grew, Romy felt herself mentally deteriorating. The strain of being attracted to a client that she could never have, combined with the dangers of Thomas Black, had become overwhelming for her.

As Romy continued down the expansive driveway, she turned to the left, remembering that she had parked to the side of a walking path adjacent to the estate property. *You're doing the right thing. You know that you could never be happy having a secret affair*, Romy told herself. But no matter how logical she wanted to be, a stronger force was crying out from inside her soul. *But if I'm doing the right thing, why is leaving Emerald breaking my heart? What if that is a sign that I should stay?*

Forging onward, Romy reached her car and opened the passenger seat, throwing her large duffle bag inside. As she moved towards the driver's seat, Romy felt a thud on the back of her head. Reeling in a daze, she tried to turn around, only to be surrounded by total darkness.

15

No, I can't let her leave—I just can't. Maybe I can catch her before she drives off. As soon as Romy walked out the front door, Emerald collapsed to the floor, sobbing profusely. She felt crazed with emotion, as though her heart was being ripped from her chest. Emerald recognized that it was unfair to try and keep Romy in her life, knowing her limitations. But a big part of her was now toying with the idea of coming out and what that might look like for her future.

Taking a few deep breaths to calm herself, Emerald gathered herself off the marble floor. She heard footsteps coming down the winding staircase. "Emerald? Is that you?" Marilyn called out. "Are you okay?"

Choking back her sniffles, Emerald replied in a shaky voice, "Um, yup, I-I'm fine. I'm okay." Quickly wiping her eyes, the actress added, "I'm going for a walk on the estate grounds. I'll be back soon."

Emerald felt a hand on her shoulder as she went for the door handle. Turning around, Emerald saw Marilyn standing there with open arms. She embraced Emerald, whispering in her ear, "I know how much you cared for her. I'm going to miss her too." Shocked, Emerald froze, as though understanding for the first time that Marilyn was privy to their trysts. *Oh my god! How did she know she means so much to me?*

As if Marilyn could read Emerald's mind, she added, "Don't worry; your secret is safe with me. But please be careful if you're going out. I don't want anything to happen to you."

Emerald bobbed her head, her face swollen from crying. Then, grabbing Marilyn's hands, she expressed her gratitude. "Thank you. Don't worry; I'll be okay. Romy gave me this before she left." Emerald showed Marilyn the buzzer, which had remained in her palm. "It's an alarm that will

signal the police as soon as I push it. I'll keep it on
me while I'm strolling around."

Appearing worried as she nodded, Marilyn
replied, "Alright. Be safe, and let me know if I can
do anything, even if it's just a nice meal, to help
you feel better." Emerald quickly kissed Marilyn
on the cheek before heading outside to clear her
head. "I will. See you in a bit."

Emerald strolled down the gravel driveway,
feeling disoriented. She hadn't felt this much grief
in her heart since her relationship with Lana had
ended. She had faked it for movie scenes, of
course, she was gifted at heartbreak scenes, but
here she was in one of her own and she didn't like
it one bit.

Emerald wasn't sure what direction she wanted
to travel, only that she desperately wanted Romy to
return. Emerald spoke aloud to herself. "I'm probably too late; I'll bet she's gone by now."

Emerald continued to walk down the path
leading to the property's edge. The warm air was
soothing, and the bright blue sky was in direct
opposition to Emerald's mood. But even in her
sadness, it felt good to be outside.

Emerald noticed Romy's vehicle in the distance
as she approached a path that deviated from her

driveway. *Oh my god, she's still here! I may have a chance after all!* But as she got closer, she noticed a second car and three unrecognizable bodies.

Slowing her pace, Emerald began to tiptoe slowly, her hand clutching the buzzer. At first, Emerald only saw the backs of heads and figures between the branches of the forested area. Then, a feeling of dread overcame her as Emerald crouched down, hoping not to be seen by anyone. While she couldn't identify the car or the people near Romy's vehicle, Emerald knew she was approaching a dangerous encounter.

As she moved slowly down the path towards Romy's vehicle, her footsteps crunched on some branches, causing the unknown heads to turn. Emerald froze in her tracks, but it was too late; she had been spotted by three men. *Oh my god, one of them is Thomas.* "Here, there she is," she heard Thomas shout.

Emerald stood up, knowing she had been caught, ready to confront the men. *But if Romy's car is there, where is she?* As she approached Romy's SUV, she noticed the Romy lying face down on the ground. Immediately, Emerald pressed the buzzer, understanding the gravity of the situation. Running towards the vehicle, Emerald screamed,

"Romy! Romy, are you okay?" She turned to face her ex-husband as the two other men surrounded Emerald. Crying out hysterically, Emerald demanded, "What happened to her? What did you do to her?"

Emerald tried to push through the men to run towards Romy, but they blocked her, with Thomas holding her arms. Then, with the two thugs beside him, Thomas squared off to face Emerald. "Listen, I don't want to hurt you. But you owe me money, Emmy."

Emerald met the terrifying rage in Thomas's eyes; she already knew Thomas had an incredible temper. Still, she struggled, calling out, "Romy! Please, say something! I need you to know you're alive. I love you!"

The two thugs snickered as Thomas tightly held on to Emerald, his hands clamping down on her wrists. "You better pay up, or you're going to end up like that dyke guard of yours."

One of Thomas's lackeys laughed cruelly as he pointed toward Romy's unconscious body. "Hah, she can't help you now, can she? Not that she was any match for one of us." He pointed a gnarly finger in Emerald's face and added, "It was pretty stupid of you to hire a female bodyguard; what a joke! Guess you're just going to have to pay up, huh?"

Thomas interrupted his associate, exerting his control. Against her will, Thomas pulled Emerald closer to him as she wrestled from his grip. "Now, listen to me. You and I will walk back up to the house, nice and calm. You are going to hold my hand like we are back in love and everything is fine." Yanking Emerald's arm harder, sneering in her ear, he continued, "We are going to walk inside and head straight up the stairs to the safe on the fourth floor. Don't think I forgot about it, bitch!"

Emerald thought fast. She knew the police were coming to the location from where she buzzed the alarm, so she wanted to keep the men beside Romy's SUV. If she could stall the thugs long enough, they would find Romy and arrest the men. But Emerald knew she was taking a chance on her life and Romy's. Emerald saw Romy's body twitch from her peripheral vision, which made her feel hopeful. *She's still alive, but the police need to be here soon!* "Okay, okay. I will. But please, I just need to see if Romy is alright. Please, I need to check." Emerald struggled against Thomas's grip in an attempt to keep the men at the location.

As she tried to pull away, the other two men

grabbed Emerald to keep her from running to the bodyguard. Thomas laughed cruelly. "Oh, is that your new girlfriend? I don't think she'll be much help, lying unconscious on the ground. Me and the boys have plans for that dyke, after I take what's mine from the safe."

As Emerald continued to struggle, she heard the faint sound of sirens in the distance. *Oh my god, they're coming!* Amidst the chaos, the actress could tell the men didn't pick up on the noise. Emerald knew she needed to stay on the trail for the police to find them. As the sirens became louder, Emerald saw the flashing red and blue lights through the trees on the path.

Suddenly, one of the men cried out, "Shit! Someone called the cops!" Thomas's eyes grew wide as he glanced between the goons and Emerald. "What the fuck, bitch? Why are the police coming?" Thomas shook Emerald roughly as the flashing vehicle pulled up on the trail. The alarm fell out of Emerald's hand, and one of the gangsters picked it up.

"Boss, she had an alarm on her this whole time!" Thomas gasped in anger, pulling out a gun from his back pocket. Putting the cold metal to Emerald's temple, he shouted, "You fucking whore!

You fucking called the cops on me? You're dead, bitch!" Emerald heard a click, knowing she was about to be shot.

"Hold it right there!" Two police officers jumped out of their vehicle, pulling out their weapons. A uniformed officer moved swiftly behind one of Thomas' associates, pulling an arm behind his back while drawing his weapon. The other cop pointed his gun at the second thug, leaving Thomas without the aid of his friends. "Drop the gun and move away from the woman. Put your hands up in the air!"

Emerald was frozen with fear; she knew she was one move away from being killed. But the officers had disarmed his help, leaving Thomas to surrender. She felt the grip around her neck loosen, hearing the gun hit the ground in a thud. Her heart pounded in her chest as one of the officers motioned for Emerald to walk toward them. To the actress, everything felt as though it was moving in slow motion. Her body felt numb as she slowly stepped away from Thomas in a stupor.

"Alright, alright, don't shoot," Emerald heard Thomas concede as he raised his hands. As the actress moved closer to the cop car, the other police officer swiftly grabbed Thomas, locking his hands behind his back with a pair of metal cuffs. Emerald looked in the back seat to see the other two men locked inside. Shaking profusely, Emerald dropped to the ground as Thomas was dragged to the vehicle to join his crew.

"Ma'am? Are you alright?" One officer crouched beside Emerald as she gasped, crying while she tried to catch her breath. "Do you need any medical attention?"

Emerald pointed at Romy's unconscious body, panicking. "Please! Help her! I think she's still alive." The policeman wrapped a blanket around the actress in an attempt to calm her down. "Here, take this. I'll get you some water. Don't worry; we have an ambulance on the way."

Through her tears, she watched an officer read the men their rights, while another went to Romy's side. Emerald's eyes were locked on Romy's body, watching intently for any more signs of movement. Emerald's body continued to shake under the blanket as she pulled the material snugly around her. Then, unable to stay still, Emerald rushed over to Romy, collapsing beside her.

As Emerald wrapped her arms around Romy, she could feel the warmth of her body and feel the rise and fall of her chest with each breath, giving her hope.

I love you. I love you. I want to be with you forever.

Then, suddenly, two paramedics arrived beside her. "I'm sorry, lady, but you'll need to move out of the way so we can put her in the ambulance."

Emerald didn't want to let go of Romy, but she knew Romy needed urgent help. "Please help her, don't let her die!" Sobbing, the police officer guided Emerald away from Romy, allowing the paramedics to attend to Romy. The actress watched an attendant slowly roll Romy over, attaching an oxygen mask to the her face. The other paramedic brought a stretcher, and the medics carefully lifted Romy's body onto the gurney. Emerald saw a smear of blood on the side of Romy's head as she exclaimed, "Oh my god, she's bleeding! I can't lose her; I just can't!"

As the paramedics brought Romy into the ambulance, an attendant asked, "Would you like to ride beside her?" Emerald sniffled, wiping her tears. "Oh, yes, please!" I want to go with her. I need to know that she is going to be okay."

"Alright, ma'am, get inside. But please, you need to remain calm. Her vital signs are stable, and her breathing is normal." The paramedic led Emerald into the back of the ambulance, allowing her to squeeze beside the gurney. "We are rushing her to Palm Bay Hospital right now."

Emerald crouched beside the bed, reaching under the blanket to grab Romy's hand. Through her tears, she whispered, "I love you, Romy. If you get through this, I swear, I'll do anything to be with you." Emerald continued to sob as the ambulance drove away, leaving the crime scene in a dust trail.

16

"Romy, Romy!" Romy could see Emerald as she desperately tried to flag her body-guard down. As Romy tried to wave to Emerald in return, her arms felt glued to her body. Alarmed, Romy looked down at her legs and feet, which seemed fused to the ground below like roots on a tree. She looked up, her eyes frozen in fear. She could tell by the sound of Emerald's voice that she was in distress.

Romy went to open her mouth to let Emerald know that she could see her. But even as her lips formed the words, no sound escaped. The women were only a few feet apart, but to Romy, it felt like miles, and the distance seemed to expand the more Romy tried to express herself. She was desperate to run to Emerald, to *save her from whatever was happening, but it was no use; Romy was slowly turning into a statue, unable to help. She was completely helpless and terrified for both her and Emerald.*

As Emerald began to fade away into the distance, a shadowy figure began to form in place of her. Romy could surmise that it was an image of a human, but the shape appeared more like a giant, square wall. Whatever the form was, it was large and menacing. Once again, Romy tried to move her body while attempting to yell, but it was useless. The human form approached closer until it overshadowed Romy completely, and Emerald was now entirely out of Romy's view.

Oh no! Is this the end? What is happening? Why can't I defend myself? *Romy's thoughts were coherent in her mind, so she knew she wasn't dead yet. But as she felt herself being swallowed up by the threatening shadow, Romy knew that it would soon be her end. Her mind cried out,* Emerald! I love you! I'm trying to save you, but I can't! I can't; I'm so sorry, I'm sorry!

In the distance of her unconscious mind, Romy began to hear a series of strange sounds, repetitive beeping, combined with static and strange voices in the background. Then, she felt her body fall down an invisible tunnel, landing with a thud.

Blinking, Romy opened her eyes. *Oh my god, I can move again! I'm not dead! Where am I?*

The first thing Romy saw as her eyes opened was bright overhead lights, blinding her vision. There seemed to be material wrapped around her, like a cocoon. Her fingers wiggled automatically, and Romy twitched, trying to comprehend her existence. Then, a familiar voice cried out, "Oh my god, she's alive!"

As her vision came into focus, Romy could see Emerald standing over her, her golden hair tousled and lovely like a halo in the light, her hazel eyes full of concern, and she felt the touch of warm fingers on her hand. Confused but ecstatic, Romy tried to answer, but her voice came out squeaky and soft. "Emerald? I thought you disappeared! Where did you go?"

An unfamiliar male voice added to the cacophony. "Good, she seems stable. Romy? Can you hear me?" Romy's sight was now fully restored. She saw Emerald, who was crying, and a man dressed in light blue scrubs. Clearing her throat, she attempted to speak again, this time more clearly. "Um, yes. Yes, I can hear you."

"I'm Doctor Bardot. You're lucky to be alive, but your vital signs are stable. You're going to be okay, but you suffered a severe concussion and various contusions." The physician continued, "Luckily, the wounds are only superficial, no broken bones. But we would like to keep you here for at least overnight, under observation, while you heal. Do you remember what happened to you?"

Romy felt confused and frightened. At this time, she had no recollection other than leaving Emerald's mansion in a fit of tears. "I-I don't think so. I remember walking down a path towards my car but can't remember anything else right now."

Gently, the doctor explained, "According to the police, you were attacked by some criminals and hit over the head. I need you to rest for now, but I'm confident the memories will return. But don't stress yourself about it. Right now, you'll need time to rest."

"Can I come closer, please?" Romy heard Emerald beg the doctor as she tried to motion Emerald closer to her bedside. The doctor conceded, "Yes, you may have some time together. But then, you'll need to leave. You're welcome to return tomorrow during visiting hours."

After a few quick tests, the doctor shut the door behind him, leaving the women alone. Emerald approached Romy's bedside and began to sob. "Oh my god, you have no idea! I thought you were dead. I tried to save you. Luckily, I had the alarm you gave me, so I was able to notify the police."

Hearing Emerald's words, Romy began to piece the incident together. Then, she exclaimed, grabbing Emerald's hand to pull her closer, "Oh wow! Okay, it's coming back to me. I remember seeing Thomas...and his gang—it was them!"

Emerald gently stroked Romy's forehead. "Yes, that's right. After you left, I couldn't bear it, so I tried to catch you before you drove away for good. I encountered Thomas and his friends. There was a struggle, but I was able to hit the alarm. The police and ambulance arrived and took you to the hospital." Emerald paused, looking deep into Romy's eyes. "I was so scared. I love you, Romy. And I don't care who knows it. In fact, I want to tell the world that I am in love with you. I can't lose you; I need you, and I want us to be together. Like, officially."

I love you too.

"So, before I woke up, I guess I was having a dream, although I didn't know it. I could hear you in the distance, and as I tried to help, my body began to freeze on the spot. I could see you fading away, and I was completely helpless." Romy was overcome with emotion. "It was the worst feeling, seeing you disappear. But, Emerald, I can't lose you either. I want to keep you safe in my arms and love you every day."

Simultaneously, the women dissolved into joyful tears, understanding how precious their love was for one another. Emerald gently cupped Romy's face in her hand and held her gaze. "Romy, I meant what I said; I want to be with you in every way. I want the world to know that I love you. I'm not afraid anymore. My heart can't bear to pay the cost of losing you."

Emerald's words filled Romy with hope. "Are you sure? I could never be the reason that you would lose your career. Of course, I also want us to be together like a couple, but the decision has to be yours." Romy blinked, wincing in pain. Still, Romy was ecstatic to have Emerald by her side. But she needed to be sure that Emerald was making the right choice for herself.

Emerald bobbed her head confidently. "Absolutely. And I have a surprise for you." Then, just as she was about to continue, Romy saw Chet, Emerald's agent, peek his head in the doorway of her hospital room. "Hey! Sorry to interrupt, ladies. Romy, are you okay?"

Romy smiled as she motioned for Chet to enter the room. "I'll be fine; it was just a little bang on the head. I'm a tough cookie, though. It will take more than that to finish me off." Emerald chuckled, exclaiming, "Oh good, you're here! Thanks for coming down. I have something important to tell you, and this needs to go public, Chet."

The agent crept into the room, sitting in a chair close to Romy's bed. "You mentioned something mysterious on the phone, so I hurried right away. Are *you* okay? I heard that Thomas attacked you! Is that true?"

Emerald glanced at Romy and shrugged. Romy nodded at the actress, encouraging her to explain. "Um, well, yes. In fact, he assaulted Romy first. But unfortunately, I wasn't aware until I found her lying beside her car. Luckily, I was able to notify the police, and they came just in time." Romy observed Emerald as she nervously cleared her throat.

"But Chet, that's not exactly what I wanted to tell you." Romy squeezed Emerald's hand as the actress continued, taking a deep breath. "Chet, I want you to hear it from me first. I am a lesbian, always have been, and I am in love with Romy. We've been having an affair since I hired her as my bodyguard. I don't want to hide my truth anymore. Romy and I are a couple."

Romy teared up upon hearing Emerald's proclamation. Her heart soared with pride, impressed at Emerald's courage and conviction. Chiming in, she validated Emerald's statement. "It's true. I know it's been hard for Emerald to be honest about her sexuality, and I'm so proud of her."

Chet's expression went from surprise to excitement. "Are you serious? Wow, what a story! Emerald, this is *huge* news! Personally, I'm so happy for the two of you. But how do you want to proceed with this?"

Emerald continued, "That's precisely why I asked you to come to the hospital. I want you to contact Lynn from P.R. I want to give a public statement that I am coming out and I want to speak openly about my past love affairs. Obviously there will be lots of women I am unable to name, but I am tired of hiding. I want the world to know the truth and that it is ok to love who you want to love." Emerald looked lovingly at Romy before adding, "And if Romy agrees, I'd like a photo taken of us so that the world knows she is my girlfriend."

Romy was floored by the news, finally grasping

that Emerald was serious about their relationship. Any physical discomfort that she was feeling had been eradicated in this moment of truth. Exhaling deeply, Romy stated, tugging on Emerald's hand, "Come here; I want to kiss you. Just be gentle!"

Emerald slowly lowered her face, brushing her soft lips against Romy's. The sensation was electric, causing goosebumps to cover Romy's arms. "Wow, this is really happening!"

Eagerly, Chet stood up. "I'll contact Lynn right away. I think we will do a TV interview for you with a big name journalist. You can then speak your truth entirely openly and tell your side of everything, including this mess with Thomas and your love for Romy. This is massive and I think it will actually be huge for your career now. It is 2023 Emerald, we live in a very different world than the one that existed when you first hit Hollywood. I can't believe it; congrats, you two! Man, Hollywood loves nothing more than a great love story." Emerald squealed with delight, holding Romy's hand. Suddenly, the group was interrupted by a uniformed policeman who knocked on the door.

"Excuse me, Emerald Crowle?" She sat up from the edge of Romy's bed. She was as beautiful as ever and Romy couldn't take her eyes off her. She couldn't believe that Emerald was with her. Like, really with her. "Yes, that's me! What's happening?"

"Hi, ma'am. I'm here to inform you that your ex-husband has been arrested and charged with assault with a deadly weapon, attempted murder and attempted kidnapping," the officer stated. He stood at attention as he continued, "His bail has been set to a million dollars, so we suspect he'll be sitting in jail until his court appearance in two months."

Romy gasped, clapping her hands together. "Oh my god, that's great news, Emmy!" Romy watched as Emerald's eyes filled with tears of gratitude. "Oh wow, I can't believe it. He's finally out of my life." The actress glanced at Romy, squeezing her hand. "Sorry, I meant *our* life."

Romy was filled with joy. Emerald was now safe and was able to live her life fully. She knew this was true love and that she and Emerald could have a real future together. "Babe, I can't wait to start our life. In fact, it's starting right now." Pulling Emerald close, Romy kissed Emerald Crowle, *the Emerald Crowle*, now her girlfriend. Any physical discomfort had completely left her body; love had cured all.

EPILOGUE
5 YEARS LATER

Emerald positioned a bouquet of tropical flowers in the center of the dining table. "Ah, perfect. That looks lovely!" Satisfied with the place settings, she returned to the kitchen to check on dinner. Tonight, she was celebrating her second wedding anniversary. Her fourth marriage, but this was the first one that was real for her. First real love. Romy Russell. While the festivities were far more low-key than Emerald had previously been accustomed to, she was happier than she had ever been in her life.

Emerald opened the oven door, taking a whiff of the baked chicken she had prepared for her and Romy, knowing the recipe was her wife's favorite dish. Knowing that she was a novice in the kitchen, Emerald had practiced a few times, wanting to perfect the recipe. It was a simple meal compared to the extravagant dishes that Emerald had enjoyed in the past. But while sophisticated restaurants could superficially impress with their opulent atmosphere and expensive price tags, these venues couldn't match the loving warmth of a home-cooked meal.

Not long after she and Romy officially became a couple, the now ex-actress began a healing journey with the help of a therapist. In addition to the trauma she faced with Thomas, with the help of Romy and her counselor, Emerald was able to get back in touch with her authentic self. Emerald recognized how vapid and superficial she had become in the movie industry for decades. Now, with Romy by her side, Emerald felt courageous; true love had empowered her. Acting was finished for her now. There was no shortage of roles that had been offered to her since she had come out, but she realized she wanted different things now.

She was considering taking on a lesbian role if the right one came up. But it would need to be one she believed in passionately. She was done acting in movies purely for the box office.

After checking on dinner, Emerald noticed the time. *Romy should be back from teaching any minute. I should bring down her gift.* She ran up the stairs to the second floor of their Renaissance-style home, which the couple purchased in Hawaii Loa Ridge's gated community. In the master bedroom, Emerald retrieved her wedding anniversary gift for Romy.

Running her finger along the Koa wood frame, Emerald smiled as she studied the photo of herself and Romy. During their honeymoon, it was taken in front of the Namaka Wellness Retreat.

Emerald barely recognized herself; she felt she had changed so much in the past five years. With a pang of nostalgia, she gathered the framed photo and a small jewelry box containing a custom peridot and black coral ring she had made especially for Romy. Emerald thought it would make a fitting gift, considering black coral was the official gem of Hawaii, which the couple had since made their home.

Just as Emerald returned to the main floor, she heard Romy enter their home. "Hey, Em! My day is finally done, and now I can relax." She rushed into the living room to embrace her wife. "Happy anniversary, my love." Then in a playfully scolding tone, Emerald added, "You'd think that a co-owner would've taken a day off on her anniversary!" Emerald was only teasing Romy; she was impressed with her partner's work ethic and passion. She wanted Romy to have something in her life that gave her purpose and enjoyment.

Romy pulled in Emerald, tightly squeezing her. "I know, babe. But I love teaching these classes, and with Marisol sick, I felt obligated to help out the team owner." Kissing Emerald lightly on the nose, Romy joked, "I thought your diva days were behind you!"

Emerald lightly swatted Romy on the arm. "Oh, shush! You know I'm only kidding. I admire how committed you are to the Wellness Center, and I think it's important that we remain active and connect with the community, *especially* as owners." She pointed towards the kitchen, adding, "If I weren't so busy watching over a hot meal in the kitchen, I would have run my Tropical Landscaping & Tiki class. But I told Lolani to cancel that session for this week."

Emerald beamed as Romy pulled her closer, kissing her neck softly. "Well, I think you made the right choice. It smells amazing in here. Did you use fresh rosemary?" Romy asked, pausing to sniff the air.

"I did! Why don't you get settled, and I'll serve us dinner in the dining room," Emerald suggested. She loved the look of seeing Romy sweaty and flushed, but she was also eager to eat. Her appetite had been robust ever since moving with Romy to Hawaii. Emerald assumed it was from a combination of clean air and their work to restore the Namaka Wellness Retreat as the new co-owners. And Emerald especially loved Romy's dedication to her women's self-defense classes. She knew it gave Romy a sense of purpose through helping people, paired with a physical workout.

After Romy showered, the couple sat to eat, surrounded by candles that Emerald artfully placed around the table. They reminisced over their early days of meeting one another, laughing at their personality differences that ultimately brought them together in marriage. Even after five years together, Emerald was still in awe of Romy's strength, beauty, and patience. And she was also surprised at her own self-growth.

"And I have you to thank you for that. Did you ever imagine us *here*, co-owning a wellness retreat?

I swear, I never saw it coming!" Emerald exclaimed as she gripped her wife's hand.

"I can't say I saw this exact scenario coming, but I *did* have a feeling that, eventually, our lives together would change. I didn't know *how*, but I knew we couldn't continue a life in the spotlight for longer. At least, I couldn't." Romy commented between bites of roasted, rosemary-flavored chicken.

"Oh, Romy, it was beyond time for me to move on, too. Well, not that I will ever be exactly low profile unfortunately, but life is much easier out here for someone like me."

"Oh, that reminds me!" Emerald had placed Romy's gifts on a chair hidden beside her. "Happy anniversary. These are for you."

Dimples formed on Romy's cheeks, and she gave Emerald a delighted grin. "Oh wow, thank you! I have something for you as well." Romy narrowed her gaze seductively. "But it's upstairs. I was going to give it to you later."

Emerald blushed. The passion between them was thriving; Romy still had a way of giving Emerald butterflies. Joking as she dramatically fanned herself, "Oh my! It sounds like your gift may be more like dessert."

"More like *you're* the dessert! But that can wait until after dinner." Romy grabbed Emerald's hand, pulling her closer. She met Romy's gaze, kissing her softly. "Okay, fair, but can you open your gift *now*? I've been waiting to give it to you all day!"

Romy chuckled, shaking her head. "Alright! I don't want to keep the princess waiting. But, no, I'm kidding; I'd love to, and thank you for thinking of me."

Emerald handed Romy the gift-wrapped parcels. "Here, start with this one." She passed the larger, rectangle-shaped present to her wife, grinning with delight. Emerald watched as Romy carefully unwrapped the package.

"Oh wow, Em!" Romy freed the present from its covering, presenting an 11x17-inch Koa wood picture frame. She ran her hand over the glass that covered the image. "This wood is absolutely gorgeous. And look at us! We look so happy outside of the retreat." Emerald observed tears forming in Romy's eyes, and she, too, was full of emotion. "That trip was such a turning point for us; this is a memory I will cherish forever."

Emerald bobbed her head. "I know, right? An incredible honeymoon combined with the perfect business opportunity. Who could've imagined that?" Romy nodded in agreement. "As soon as we arrived at Namaka, I felt like it was home. After meeting Mia and spending those few days with her and her wife, everything felt like it was meant to be."

"Oh, I loved Mia; they were so cute together. I trusted her immediately; her energy was amazing. And I can't believe the deal we got! Namaka Wellness Retreat is an incredible venture." She squeezed Romy's hand and added, "I have so many ideas for the place."

Romy replied gently, "I know how much you care about the center. But for now, don't get overwhelmed. Your garden and landscaping classes seem to keep you busy enough. I want you to focus on yourself too, babe."

Emerald cherished Romy's support, and she knew her wife was correct. Thomas was inevitably sentenced to 25 years in prison, although the trial and its publicity had taken a toll on Emerald. But she found solace living in Hawaii and co-owning Namaka. In particular, Emerald discovered horticulture eased her anxiety and elevated her soul. It took a few years for Emerald to heal from the violent situation fully, but luckily, with the love of her wife and through a change in location, she was able to find peace and happiness.

"Okay, open the second present now." Emerald excitedly clapped her hands together. She passed Romy a tiny, gift-wrapped box. Romy grinned, exclaiming, "Babe, you're spoiling me. I thought we agreed not to get extravagant with the gifts."

Half-joking, Emerald rolled her eyes to the ceiling. "I *know*, but come on. You know I had to get you *something!* I love you so much, and you know my gift-giving habit." Romy winked at Emerald and fiddled with the box, revealing the custom-designed ring.

Romy gasped. "Oh my god, it's *beautiful!* I love peridot so much. Thank you, so much."

Emerald reached to take Romy's hand. "Here, I'd like to put it on you." Romy presented her fingers so that Emerald could slide the ring next to Romy's wedding band. Her wife admired the stones as Emerald spoke. "I wanted to have something made that symbolizes our journey, and that celebrates our new surroundings. As you know, the black coral signifies the mystery of the ocean, and the peridot symbolizes strength and balance."

Romy studied the ring, marveling at its reflective qualities. "I think your strength is amazing, and I feel like I bring us balance. We're different in the best ways that complement our relationship."

Emerald's eyes lit up. "Exactly! And the black coral represents our future, all of the mysteries and adventures that are in store for us." Romy gazed into Emerald's eyes.

"It's perfect, just like you." The women passionately kissed, leaning over their dinner plates before getting up to clear the table. In the absence of domestic service, Emerald and Romy were left to tidy the kitchen themselves, although Emerald didn't mind. In fact, she found that she *enjoyed* cleaning up with Romy. For the first time in her life, she felt that her house was a real home, and creating a cozy and loving space with Romy filled Emerald with pride and joy.

"Oh, I forgot to tell you," Emerald mentioned while drying her hands on a dish towel. "I spoke to Marilyn this morning after you left to teach at the center." Romy turned to face Emerald, appearing concerned. "Oh yeah? How is she? How did the surgery go?"

"She's doing fine," Emerald reassured her wife. "Apparently, the hip replacement was smooth, with no issues. She's at home now, and her daughter is taking care of her. But she sounds like she is in great spirits!"

"Good, I'm so happy to hear that. I thought Marilyn may have been out of the hospital by now. In fact, I was going to call her tomorrow morning. How is she settling into the property?" Romy asked.

Emerald chuckled. "I think she finally feels at home now that the initial shock has worn off. She mentioned that she's been decorating the back patio. I think she enjoys those little projects."

Romy giggled. "I can still remember the look on her face when you took off the blindfold. I was worried she was going to have a heart attack! She was just so amazed. It was such a cool thing to see."

A laugh escaped from Emerald. "I know! I almost cried seeing her expression. But she deserved that house more than anyone. And I know you didn't feel like it was right for you. We needed a fresh start, and Marilyn needed a break. She's taken care of me for most of my adult life. And I wanted her to retire in style!"

"That's the one thing I've always loved about you—your generosity. You could've made millions from the mansion. And considering all of the expenses related to the retreat, it's not like we couldn't have used that towards the business," Romy commented. "But you absolutely made the right choice. Marilyn is family."

"Honestly, what's millions if you can't enjoy it with the people you love? I know we have some serious repairs to look into, but I don't care. I've been wealthy for most of my life, and neither the money nor the success meant anything before meeting you."

Emerald looked around their kitchen, which was considerably smaller than the mansion's dining area. Nevertheless, she adored the quirky Hawaiian knick-knacks and tiki designs that decorated the space and the collection of dishware that she shared with Romy. The room was cozy and eclectic; the energy of their relationship warmed the environment.

The couple retired to the living room to digest and relax. Both Emerald and Romy planned to be onsite at the retreat in the morning, so they were grateful to enjoy downtime with each other. As Emerald snuggled with Romy on their oversized, white leather couch, she heard her phone ring from the kitchen.

"Weird! I wonder who could be calling this

late." Emerald stood up to retrieve her device. While she still kept in touch with past contacts who were meaningful, her phone had become quieter over the years. Then, seeing the calling ID, she noticed it was her agent.

Emerald carried the phone back into the living room and exclaimed, "Hi, Chet! I haven't heard from you in a few months. How are you?" She listened intently as Chet described an opportunity, his voice full of excitement.

"Hmmm, mmm. Okay, I see." Emerald's eyes grew wide as she signaled to Romy. She wasn't expecting this news, and it caught her off guard. "Wow, it certainly is! Thanks so much. Yes, I'll speak to Romy about it right now and let you know."

Romy sat up straight. "What is it? You look surprised." Emerald sat down beside her wife, putting a hand on her knee. Looking at Romy, she explained, "So, apparently, Chet was contacted by Netflix, and they want to do a documentary series about us."

Romy appeared confused. "About *us*? What do you mean? Like, about the retreat?"

Emerald shook her head. "No, no. Like, they want to do a series about how our relationship began and my coming out story. And, my secret lesbian history and all that. Obviously I did the initial TV interview and that has inspired them to want to make a series."

"Oh wow, that sounds interesting! What do you think?" Romy asked. Furrowing her brow, Emerald felt uncertain about the opportunity. Over the past five years, Emerald had slowly extricated herself from the industry, instead putting energy into the Namaka Wellness Retreat. She knew that her name would be immortalized in Hollywood, so these days, Emerald was cautious about being involved in film projects that drained her emotionally.

"I don't know." Emerald laid her head on Romy's shoulder. "You and I already went through a media frenzy when our story first came out. And that was a lot, remember?" Then, glancing up at Romy, Emerald added, "And I keep thinking about what my therapist said about maintaining my boundaries and personal space."

Romy laced her fingers around Emerald's, petting her hair. "Yes, I remember. It was definitely a crazy time for us. And it was hard for me as well because I wasn't used to being in the spotlight at all." Romy shook her head, running her hand through her glossy brown hair. Emerald loved Romy's new haircut with the sides shaved. *God, my wife is so freakin' hot! How did I get so lucky?*

Emerald lightly touched the longer pieces of Romy's hair while rubbing her back with a hand. "That's what I'm getting at. I adore our love story; I'm even grateful for Thomas' violent behavior because, without him, I never would have met you. But it's still a lot to process, especially when the public is involved."

Romy nodded, pausing for a few moments of silence. Emerald heard her take a breath before offering, "There is one positive aspect to the offer, though. Imagine how impactful the series could be for other gay women living in the closet. Do you remember the letters and emails we received when our story came out? The whole situation felt bigger than just our own story." Then, turning to face Emerald, Romy added, "If the series could be helpful to our community, maybe it's worth considering it?"

Emerald hemmed and hawed. She felt slightly doubtful, but Emerald knew it was also because she had become jaded from her longtime career. She had learned long ago that profits ruled the TV and movie industry; providing a public service to communities was never the goal. But at the same time, Emerald knew that Romy had a point.

"Hmmm, maybe. I love the idea of the series inspiring others to be brave and empowered by their identities and sexual orientation. And if that is something that could come out of this project, we *should* consider it. But I think we should have a meeting with Chet and the producer to understand the objectives." Emerald bit her lip as she opened her mind to the possibility.

"I have a thought. Why don't we write a proposal about our goals regarding the potential series? That way, we can provide an outline and perimeters. Because, like you, I also don't want to feel exploited," Romy suggested.

Suddenly, Emerald was hit with an inspiring idea; it was something she had always wanted to try, but until now, she had not found an opportunity. Exclaiming, Emerald squealed. "I know! Why don't I ask to co-write the series myself? I already have decades of experience understanding scripts, and I've worked closely with every top director in Hollywood!"

Romy's eyes grew wide, matching Emerald's energy. "Oh my god, that's a great idea! That way, we can have some control over the narrative. And you can explore something new within your field."

Romy smiled to herself. This was Emerald through and through, used to getting what she wanted, complete confidence that she could do anything and Romy loved that about her.

"Wow, okay, I'm excited now! This is definitely something I can do. But, of course, we still need to meet with the producer. But yes, I think that's the perfect solution." Emerald stood from the couch. "I'm going to call Chet right now." Grabbing her phone, she dialed her agent's number, reaching him on the first ring.

Emerald kept an eye on Romy as she shared their idea of writing the script for the Netflix series. Emerald also shared her hesitations, negotiating the offer as a way to portray their love story and her life story authentically. As the conversation continued, Emerald grinned, thrilled to hear Chet's positive response; she couldn't wait to tell Romy the news.

As Emerald said goodbye, Romy stood up to meet Emerald, touching her elbow. "Well? What did he say?"

Beaming, Emerald replied, "Chet *loves* the idea! He can't approve it, of course, but he said he'll speak to the director and plan a meeting with us and the producer. I know Chet will support this; he thinks it's the perfect solution."

Excitedly, the couple embraced one another, giggling with joy. Romy cupped Emerald's face, bringing her close. Emerald closed her eyes as Romy's warm lips met hers. She was the happiest she had ever been, and with Romy by her side, their future would be better than any Hollywood ending.

VIP READERS LIST

Hey! Thank you so much for reading my book. I am honestly so very grateful to you for your support. I really hope you enjoyed it.

If you enjoyed it, I would love you to join my VIP readers list and be the first to know about freebies, new releases, price drops and special free *hot* short stories featuring the characters from my books.

You can get a FREE copy of Her Boss by joining my VIP readers list : https://BookHip.com/MNVVPBP

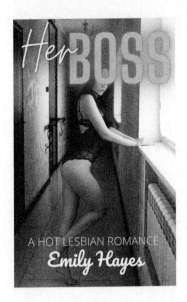

Meg has had a crush on her hot older boss the whole time she has worked for her. Could it be that the fantasies aren't just in Meg's head? https://BookHip.com/MNVVPBP

Thank you so much for reading this one. I am, as always, super grateful to you for supporting my writing career.

If you enjoyed this series, why don't you check out my super popular CEO series?

Can the right woman be enough to thaw the Ice Queen's heart?

This is an Age Gap, Ice Queen, CEO Romance. It is hot and

steamy, sweet and loving and always with a Happy Ever After.

Eva Perez is the CEO of one of the biggest and most successful companies in her industry in the US. She has everything she could ever need or want in life. She is confident she doesn't need a girlfriend to complete her.

Most women fall at Eva's feet, so when a young woman turns up for an interview with her, who seems completely unphased by her power, Eva is intrigued.

Madison is captivating and exciting to Eva and sparks fly between them right from the start.

Will Madison ever be able to melt Eva's frosty heart?

Escape into this hot and exciting Age Gap, Ice Queen romance today.

mybook.to/TCEO

Printed in Great Britain
by Amazon

43381198R00119